Maintenance & Management

Indie Sparks

Twice Shy Publishing

A Note from Indie

Welcome home to The Nouveau!
If any part of this book reads like wish
fulfillment to you, you're welcome. It was
not an accident. I didn't miss that or
overlook it or fail to realize that any
particular act or moment might not have
happened exactly that way in real life.
I wrote fiction on purpose.

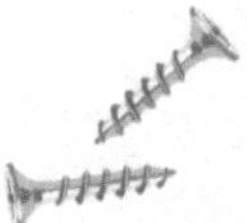

And I hope you enjoy it on purpose.
Let's leave the real world behind,
get naughty in risky places,
and fall stupid in love!
Anything can happen at The Nouveau.

xoxo,
Indie

Content Disclosure

This book contains content intended for mature readers, including profanity, consumption of alcohol, mention of past DV (not between the main characters), exhibitionism/voyeurism, and non-disciplinary spanking.

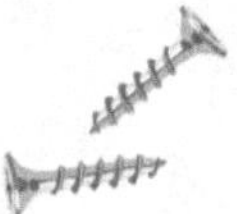

If you suffer from arachnophobia or ophidiophobia, please note that there is a scene featuring an unseen spider and many scenes featuring a very visible pet snake.
Please exercise care and caution when choosing to read.

Landry

"There is fuck all chance of me wearing this! Nobody said anything about new shirts."

I look up at the man waving the uniform shirt over my desk. He's got the fabric clutched in his fist like it insulted his mother. Damn, he's tall. He'd be tall even if I weren't looking up at him from my desk—a desk that just officially became mine five minutes ago. As a property manager, having to deal with upset people isn't unusual, but facing the first tirade on my first day before my first cup of coffee? Too much.

"And he's not wearing it either." Mr. Tall, Dark, and Angry jerks his head toward a younger, meeker blonde guy, who's followed him inside but stayed back a few feet. And then he drops the shirt on my desk like he's dropping a microphone. It lands softly and lays between us in a limp heap. I bet he saw that going differently in his head.

I lift the fabric to see what's wrong with it. No misprint on the property name. The word maintenance is spelled correctly. "Is it the buttons?" I ask. "Did you never learn to master them as a child?"

"I can navigate buttons just fine, sweetheart." His hazel-eyed gaze drops to the buttons on my shirt as he says it. Oh, I've got news for this asshole: those artistically tatted and exquisitely muscled arms might allow him to get away with treating women that way in a bar, but this is a workplace.

"Okay, this misogynistic bullshit stops now!" I'm on my feet and around my desk with a business card in my hand, shaking it at him the same way he shook that shirt at me. "My name's not sweetheart!" I thrust the card in his direction. "Maybe this will help."

"I see two last names here." His voice is far less combative than before, but the corners of his mouth look like he's trying to combat a smile. "Are you Landry Channing or Channing Landry?"

"The name is printed correctly. Landry. Channing. Your new manager."

"Yeah, well, I'm the maintenance supervisor, Landry. I'm my own manager." He jerks his head toward the younger guy again. "And his."

Carina's head swivels between us like she's watching a tennis match from her own desk. As if it wasn't going to be hard enough for a leasing agent to get a new manager and whole new maintenance department without this level of nonsense.

"Hold up," I say. "I didn't catch your name before you launched into your tantrum."

"Vaughn Sawyer and that's—"

"I'm sorry, but I heard two last names there. Are you Vaughn Sawyer or Sawyer Vaughn?"

His smile breaks through, but his eyes narrow into a menacing glare. If he thinks he can intimidate me, he's got another think coming. I won't be bullied, not even by a man with hands that look like he could easily pin both my wrists in one. *What? No. Stop that! Stop looking at his hands. Don't look at his chest either, even if it is practically eye-level when you're standing three feet away and broad enough to block your view of the entire lobby.*

"The name was correct as I said it. Vaughn Sawyer. Maintenance supervisor."

"Okay, well, when you're done impressing yourself with your title, you can tell me what exactly is wrong with this shirt." I reach back and grab it off my desk, holding it up so he can point out what I'm missing.

"The color."

"Burgundy?"

"Fancy name for dark pink," he says.

"It's magenta," Carina interjects. "It's the Pantone color of the year."

Her slightly defensive tone tells me she had input on this particular feature of The Nouveau's rebranding. My eyes cut toward

Vaughn to convey he'd better tread lightly here. After all, she's the only staff member who knows anything about this place. We need her.

Vaughn takes a measured breath, and our eye contact feels electric for a moment, before I force myself to break it. "Great color," he says. "If you work in a damn wine bar. When I interviewed, the maintenance guys were wearing regular blue work shirts. Last week, we wore blue shirts. Nobody said anything about changing them to wine. Or magenta, whatever." He half-glances at Carina. "No offense."

"Listen," I say, "we both know the owners just spent a fortune on renovation and rebranding. Asking for new shirts because you don't like the color is a frivolous request, at best. And as much as it pains me to compliment you right now, this will actually look really good with your dark hair. Plus, it will make your eyes pop. Trust me."

He sighs. I hear the defeat he's about to accept, but I also know he's going to bitch about these shirts until they wear out and we can reorder.

"Why can't we just keep wearing the blue ones? Why'd you have to change the shirts? You couldn't think of another way to make your mark on day one?"

"Those shirts were ordered long before I got here. You want to yell at somebody about them, call up the owners." I already know I'll offer to switch the uniform shirts to a color he likes better when the time comes, provided I'm not doing hard time for his murder by then. His chances of survival aren't looking so good on day one.

I look to the younger man. "Do you have any complaints to register?"

He shakes his head no, barely looking up from his feet.

"It's okay, Holden." I give him a friendly smile. "You can speak. We've all got to learn to work together."

"You already know my name?"

"I knew both your names before you entered the office. I'd be a pretty crappy manager if I didn't even know my employees' names."

Vaughn scoffs. "Don't go patting yourself on the back just yet, swee—"

Carina gasps. I mean, yeah, bold of him to even *think* about calling me sweetheart again, but her reaction seems extreme. If she can't even handle this level of confrontation, I don't know how she's lasted four years dealing with tenants.

"Whoa!" Holden yells.

I turn to Carina for clues, and find her staring at the carpet. "Dammit, Lolita." she says. "You scared the shit out of me."

The brightest orange-and-red-patterned snake I've ever seen is slithering between our desks. Oh, hell no!

I've somehow scooted right up next to Vaughn and am now inching my way around his solid frame to position him between me and the snake, accidentally brushing my boobs across his arm as I go. This is no time to be leaving space for Jesus. Or snakes. "Where did that come from?" I manage to choke out once I'm safely behind his body.

Carina smiles. "It's just Lolita. She belongs to Vonnie."

I slap the back of his head. "That thing is yours?"

"No," Carina says. "It belongs to Vonnie, the tenant. One of the original two?" She looks at me like I should know what she means. "Vonita Viper? Unit 320?"

Now I feel like I should know what she means, too. But I have no clue who she's talking about.

The exterior door opens an older woman, who looks to be in her seventies with hair that nearly matches the vibrant colors of the snake's skin, whisks into the lobby, yelling, "Lolly girl, are you in here socializing again?"

"She's introducing herself to the new manager, Vonnie," Carina calls, as if this snake visiting the office is a normal occurrence.

"Come here, you little tramp." Without hesitation, the woman bends down, picks up the bright snake, and lets it wrap around her slim waist. She cradles its head in her hand and coos at it. That thing has to be four feet long.

Vaughn steps forward for a closer look. "She's a beauty," he says.

"Why, so are you, handsome." The aging redhead steps back to take him in from head to toe, and back up again. "My, oh, my. Forty years ago, I'd have been knocking other performers off the stage to shake my tassels for you, honey."

"Miss Vonnie was a burlesque performer." Carina strokes the snake's head with two fingers. "A star."

What in the roadside carnival hell is happening here?

"Her stage name was Vonita Viper."

"That's right, darlin'. I always danced better with one of my babies wrapped around me." She rubs the snake's head on her face. "There is just nothing as sensual as a snake." She rotates her hips as she says it, creating waves in the fabric of her cerulean and coral silk caftan. The pattern looks like an abstract painting with swirls and swooshes that make it hard to tell where one shape ends and another begins. This tiny slip of a woman isn't lost in it, though; it would take more than some extra fabric to hide a personality that big. "My serpents made me fearless. And they made me a helluva lot of money, too!" She throws her head back and cackles. Her beaded drop earrings sway to and fro.

She wears her thinning, shoulder-length hair in loose curls. As I look at her, I can imagine it thick and shiny in her younger days. I'm undecided whether red might've been her natural shade, but I bet she always kept it red. It's her color. Bright red fingernails rake through her curls in an unmistakably flirty move. She is smitten with my lead maintenance man. Looks as if she'd like to make him her leading man in every possible way.

Oh, this could actually get quite amusing. I'm tempted to pull up a chair and see just how far she takes it. But there's that neon-carrot-colored viper between us, and that's enough to make me want to run for the parking garage.

Holden steps closer to Vonita and her viper. "That's a sunglow, right?"

"Is a sunglow venomous?" I ask, still glued to the spot on the carpet where Vaughn abandoned me for a better look at a snake.

"No, it's just a corn snake," Holden assures me. "They won't hurt you." He looks in awe of the creature. "That's a wicked bright morph."

I have no idea what language he's speaking, but I would most definitely like the bawdy old lady to take her wicked corn snake back to her apartment now. Or she could donate it to the zoo. I'm in full support of that option.

She holds the snake out so Holden can take his turn admiring it, but she never takes her eyes off Vaughn. "You are one tall drink of water, aren't you? What's your name, honey?"

"I'm Vaughn, the new maintenance supervisor."

"Be still my heart! A Vonnie for Vonnie." Her hips gyrate again. "I can't help but notice you're not wearing a ring either. It must be my lucky day."

"No ma'am, no ring." He tries, but he can't hide the cringe in his voice. He hates that she called him Vonnie, and I am living for it. "It's actually Vawwwwn," he says, enunciating with far too much emphasis as he drags it out, "not Von." He really shouldn't smile like that if he's trying to discourage her. I can already tell this woman requires blunt communication if you want to dissuade her from anything.

"Mm, mm, mmm. Well, Vawwwwn," she says with an exaggerated southern drawl, "I guess you're the one I'll need to call if my plumbing needs any attention."

"Me or Holden here. He's also maintenance."

Vonnie turns her head to look at the young man appreciating her snake with wide eyes, but she quickly looks back at Vaughn. "Oh, honey, I think the cord might still be attached to that one. I need a more mature handyman to check off my honey-do list."

Okay, this is too much second-hand embarrassment to be enjoyable, even for me. "Vonnie, does Lucy get out of her cage often?"

"Cage? Snakes don't live in cages. When she's not with me, she's in her habitat."

Yeah, well, she wasn't with you or in her habitat when she came slithering in here. "So, she came down with you, but somehow got away? And you didn't notice?"

"She's a free spirit. We all like to stray a little now and then, feed our wanderlust. Or whatever lust." She winks at Vaughn.

Carina's eyes are wild, imploring me to shut up. I get the message, but I can't let this go unaddressed. Snakes can't roam freely around the property!

"You haven't even bothered to introduce yourself," Ms.Viper says, as she looks me over like I'm an uninvited party guest.

"You're right. My apologies. I'm Landry Channing, the new manager."

"Landry." she repeats my name back like it's heavy, falling from her mouth attached to a cinderblock. It lands with a thud at my feet. "Well, I guess your parents wanted to be sure they didn't raise no free spirit then, didn't they?"

I feel my shoulders square and stiffen, but I keep the smile on my face. "It was my grandmother's maiden name."

"Oh, that was an unfortunate choice. It's been my experience when you go putting last things first, life is prone to fuck you often, lick you never." She gives me what might be a sympathetic smile. "I certainly hope that hasn't been the case for you, sweetie."

Holden looks like he's not sure he heard her correctly. Even Vaughn appears shocked. Carina laughs. "You and your sayings, Vonnie. Never change."

"You know I won't." With that, she holds her snake closer and sashays out of the office, singing "At Last," but instead of her *love* coming along, it's her *Vawwwwn* that has come along.

Her final words to me hang in the air like an ominous prediction. "So, she's one of two?" I ask.

"Yep," Carina says. "The original two. The last remaining original tenants from when The Nouveau opened in 1980. They've changed units to allow for remodels and renovations over the years, but they've never moved out."

"Is the other woman as eccentric as Vonita Viper?" I ask.

"The other original tenant is a man. Autry McDaniel. Nothing like Vonnie. He is a widower, very buttoned up and proper, but he means well; you just have to get to know him."

"They hate each other, don't they?"

"Either that, or they're madly in love. It's hard to tell sometimes."

Vaughn smiles at me. "How about I agree to keep Mr. McDaniel happy, and you handle Vonnie?" He says it like it's some form of peace offering.

"That woman hates me. Besides, I wouldn't know where to begin with her plumbing problems, Vawwwwn."

Holden pumps his fist. "Yes, I knew this job was going to kick ass. Snakes and a wacky old lady, and it's only day one!"

We all stare at him. "I'm working on a screenplay," he says. "I was hoping this place might offer some inspiration for characters. At this rate, it may generate a complete cast and a whole three-act outline by Friday."

"Well, since we're all here," I say. "I guess this is as good a time as any for our first staff meeting."

My whole staff groans, an act that confirms I am officially the manager of The Nouveau, newly renovated, but apparently long-storied, luxury living inside the Loop. I can't wait to see where this job takes me.

Vaughn

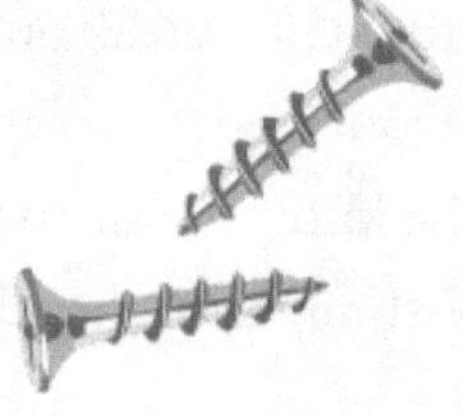

THE LAST DAMN THING I need is a manager who looks like little miss Landry Channing, with that thick, shiny, golden hair my fingers are itching to sink into, and an ass I wish she'd kept in her chair because now that I've gotten a glimpse of her curvy backside, my eyes are going to seek it out every chance they get.

And she's got an attitude like she thinks she's ten feet tall and bullet-proof, but snakes obviously scare the shit out of her. Ready to kick ass and take names until she needs a safe place to hide. Just my type.

Except she can't be more than mid-twenties, at the oldest. Too. Damn. Young. And *technically*, my boss. Not that I'll ever concede that in front of her.

I hope she doesn't think she's going to take up our whole morning with this little staff meeting. I've got work to do—namely, finishing out the make-ready on her apartment so she can move in. Right across the hall from me.

Suddenly, the free apartment perk of this job doesn't seem so incredible. Nobody gets to live onsite for free anymore. Some places don't even give the staff a break on the rent these days. This isn't the first time I've wondered if I accepted this job way too fast. What the hell could she know about running an entire property at her age, anyway? With my luck, her daddy is probably one of the owners. All the more reason to keep things strictly professional between us.

"Vaughn and Holden, have y'all familiarized yourselves with the property yet?" *Oh, get a load of that school teacher voice. That's cute.*

"We started last week," I remind her. "We know our way around." It's one building with eight floors and less than two-hundred units. Is she serious with that shit? She's the one who wouldn't be able to tell one floor from the next yet.

"I'm aware of your hire dates. Some of us had to finish our commitment to a prior job before we could start." She straightens her shoulders. Guess I struck a nerve.

"What I was going to ask was if you have any questions that you need me to pass on to the owners."

"She's been here for four years." I nod at Carina. "I imagine she can answer most questions about the property. She didn't let us down once last week."

Carina smiles, obviously happy to have her status as the only long-term employee recognized. I return the smile. It's good to have an ally. This ain't my first rodeo.

Holden pipes up. "I have a question."

"Go ahead," Landry says, trying not to let it show I've gotten to her, but she can't stand me, which is for the best. For both of us.

"Well, it seems like a lot for a property to get a new manager and all new maintenance staff at once. So, I was just wondering what happened to the people who had these jobs before us?"

I'd been curious, but not young and dumb enough to ask. Holden pulled it off just fine. I wait for Landry to spout some bullshit about how that's not our concern, and all we need to worry about is doing our jobs to the best of our abilities. She probably listens to motivational speakers in her car. Before she can start, Carina jumps at the chance to fill us all in on the property gossip.

"I can't believe they didn't tell y'all what happened. Okay, so, the manager and the maintenance supervisor were dating. Not like everyone didn't know, but two years ago, they had to start keeping it quiet because of that stupid non-fraternization policy that came with the new owners."

This the first I'm hearing of this policy. I'm not going to fraternize with anybody here, but it's for my own damn reasons, not because of some company policy. I'm a grown-ass man. I fraternize whenever, wherever, and however I want. I didn't sign anything saying otherwise. Not that it matters.

"Anyway, they finally decided to get married, and they thought when they told the owners it would be fine. Because you know, no longer dating and trying to pretend they weren't both living in the manager's apartment." Carina looks at me and laughs. "That's why your apartment looked barely lived in, Vaughn. It really was barely lived in."

Landry looks as shocked as I am to hear about this. "They got fired for getting married?"

"Yep. Although they'd have gotten fired for dating a long time ago if the owners had ever found out."

"What about the other maintenance guy?" I ask.

"He was the manager's nephew so he made a big show out of quitting in solidarity. Honestly, he didn't do much work to begin with."

My eyes find Landry's, and I suddenly want to get out of here with her for a while. Just to talk, to find out if she was made aware of any other company policies I might need to know about. The owners were so anxious to fill the position, I'm starting to worry about what else might've gotten glossed over in the rush.

Holden nods and stares off into space. I know he's thinking about how he can fit this into his screenplay. He and I are going to have to have a talk later about all that daydreaming he does. He looks up suddenly and asks, "Do the owners come around much? And if so, do you have pictures of them or something so we can recognize them? I was hired by an agency."

I was hired by an agency, too. And if Landry's family doesn't own this place, I bet she was as well.

Carina looks down at her desk like maybe she doesn't want to talk about this anymore. The phone rings, and she snaps it up immediately. "Thank you for calling The Nouveau. This is Carina. How may I help you?"

I send Holden up to Landry's future residence to start hanging her new blinds. "I'll be up in a few."

After he's out of earshot, and before Carina gets off the phone, I kneel down next to Landry at her desk and keep my voice low. "Any chance you want to share a few beers after work and talk about this place?"

"Yeah. Where do you want to meet?"

"The roof."

She points to the ceiling. "Here?"

"We're the only one who have access. No chance a tenant will be sitting nearby and overhear anything, but they might if we go somewhere in public."

"Right. That makes sense. I'll be up as soon as we close."

"See you then."

Did I just invite this gorgeous, entirely off-limits woman to meet me on the roof afterhours? So much for keeping my distance. But we really can't go anywhere in public to talk about work. The only tenant I know for sure I could recognize off the property so far is Vonnie.

The roof is the best spot. Totally private. Just me, her, and a couple beers. Teambuilding. Under the stars. Strictly business.

Landry

WHAT A FIRST DAY. I've never been so glad to see six o'clock roll around in my life. I expected some of the tenants might pop in to meet me, but if today's bunch was any indication of what's to come for the rest of the week, I definitely should've asked for more vacation time.

I'm used to working at a luxury property. I know how demanding people can be when they're paying premium rent prices, but damn. The complaints ranged from the door on the parking garage being broken more often than it's working (typical) to the pattern of carpet in the hallways on their floor being tacky, not classy like the carpet on the fourth floor (not typical). I didn't even know each floor had a different carpet. Carina says it was done to help residents recognize if they are on the right floor as soon as the elevator doors open. I guess looking at the little lit-up numbers would be too much trouble.

A beer sounds so good right now, I don't even care that I'm about to be alone with Vaughn, who I haven't seen since this morning when we scheduled this rooftop rendezvous.

Roof access is through a door at the end of the hallway between Vaughn's apartment and mine. Our units are removed from the other tenants who live on the top floor by a series of storage closets and equipment rooms. In fact, we have the only two apartments in this whole section of the hallway. The rest of the units are all around the corner, back toward the elevators. This floor has the largest units, so there are fewer of them up here overall. We're sort of secluded in the corner though, just me and him, right across the hall from each other.

As I walk toward my apartment, I wish I was already moved in. It'd be nice to be able to change into more comfortable clothes, specifically more comfy shoes. I meant to ask Vaughn to confirm my unit would be ready by the weekend as promised, but things went a little haywire once the snake showed up. A lot of what I wanted to say this morning got forgotten.

I pause at my door and trace the numbers with my fingers. 8-2-0. Four more days of my cross-town commute, and then I'll live where I've wanted to be since I moved to Houston over three years ago. *I did it!*

This was my fantasy growing up in my small, mid-dle-of-nowhere hometown. It still seems unreal, but I love everything about living in this city: the diversity of the people and the cultures, the restaurants, the museums—hell, I don't even mind the traffic. As my fingers circle the zero once more, a door opens behind me, and I jump.

Vaughn laughs. "Sorry, didn't mean to scare you."

I turn to see him exiting his apartment with a beer already in his hand. He hasn't changed clothes either. "It's okay. I figured you'd already be on the roof."

He holds up his beer. "I've got more of these on ice up there." And then he tips his bottle toward my door. "It's ready, by the way."

"My apartment?"

"Yeah."

"I was told by Friday."

"Well, I got it done by Monday. You'll find I generally exceed expectations."

It's not my fault my eyes instantly flit lower on his body. His tone was so suggestive. I'm not sure if he did it on purpose or not, but any woman alive would've initially thought he was referring to his abilities off-the-clock. It wasn't what he said, it was the way he said it, all sultry and teasing, nowhere near the defensive, grouchy way he'd said everything this morning. Stunned by my own response, I yank my gaze back up immediately. "Well, now I have to see it before we go to the roof!"

His expression becomes unreadable, and I panic, thinking maybe he really was talking about exceeding some other type of expectation, and now he's surprised by my enthusiasm. When his hand reaches for the front of his jeans, I suck in an audible breath. He looks like he's trying really hard not to smile as his hand continues to his front pocket and pulls out a key. *Way to go, Landry. Now he either thinks you're ridiculously naïve or embarrassingly horny. But also, what the hell is he doing with my key in his pocket?*

"You have a key to my apartment?"

"We literally just finished up in here thirty minutes ago. Here. You do the honors."

Our fingers touch as I take the key from him, and I swear it feels like he holds on for a beat before he lets go.

I turn the key in the lock, and push open the door to my top-floor, luxury apartment. He would laugh if he knew what a fairytale moment this feels like to me. The building is over forty-years-old, and compared to the amenities and security features of the newer properties that surround it, its luxury is fairly modest. But it is beautiful and the renovations make it feel modern.

It's so much bigger than any apartment I could afford if it didn't come with the job. The size of the units is the biggest draw at The Nouveau. Those newer, fancier places don't come with this kind of square footage. Even the first seven floors here have some of the biggest floorplans you can get in this zip code.

Stepping across the threshold, I pivot my gaze to take in the full view: gleaming new countertops and sleek cabinets in the kitchen, real wood floors and modern light fixtures. There's even a section of the downtown skyline visible through the open blinds that lead out to my small balcony. It's partially obscured, but I can see enough glass and lights from here that it feels like I'd be able to watch the people moving inside the buildings if I took a few more steps.

I know they're too far away for that, but my heart is close to bursting from happiness right now. All the stress of my first day on the job combusts into confetti of hearts and flower petals, and I can't resist spreading my arms and twirling just once.

Vaughn closes the door behind him and breaks the magic. He reaches for the dimmer switch by the front door and turns the lights up to maximum brightness. "Wow," I say, "that's a lot of light."

"Right?" He laughs, turning it back down to a level that won't blind pilots of passing planes. "I don't know why they have every fixture attached to the dimmer, but if you keep it lower and just add a lamp where you want more light, it's easier on the eyes."

"Thanks. Speaking of the brightness, that shirt does look a lot more magenta now than it did in the office."

"You should see it sunlight."

"I promise we'll switch the color when it's time to reorder."

"That may be sooner than you think. Accidents happen when you're fixing things. Shirts get torn so easily." He tugs at the shoulder seam. "And this fabric is pretty thin."

I laugh because it's not, but I know all his shirts are going to be mysteriously ruined soon. I'm actually looking forward to seeing how creative he makes their destruction.

"Go ahead," he says, nodding toward my hallway. "Check out the rest. If you can get me a punch list by Wednesday, we can probably have it all taken care of before you move in on Saturday."

"Do you think it'd be okay if I started bringing over boxes during the week?"

"I don't know who's going to stop you."

"Right." Why am I asking his permission? I flip on the light in the smaller bedroom and the bare walls halt me in my tracks. "Hey, Vaughn! When are the bookshelves going in?"

He comes down the hall, looking like I asked when the spaceship was landing instead. "What are you talking about?"

"I asked for a wall of floor-to-ceiling bookshelves in this room."

"And someone approved that?"

"Yeah, they said it was no problem."

"Nobody told me anything about any bookshelves. Where are they?"

"That's what I'm asking you." I gesture at the blank walls.

"No, I mean where are these shelves that you want installed?"

"Oh, shit. I wonder if that's what they thought I was saying, that I'd provide the shelves and just needed you to put them together. But no, I meant permanent bookshelves."

"You actually asked for floor-to-ceiling bookshelves, as in *built-in* bookshelves?"

"We offer an office conversion for the smaller bedroom. It's an option for this floorplan. I just wanted to upgrade it a little."

"The option is for a few shelves and base cabinets that can be removed if the next tenant wants to use it as a bedroom, not floor-to-ceiling built-ins. Do you want a ladder on a rail, too?"

"Oh, my god, that would make it perfect. I'm going to use this room as my library."

"How many books do you own?"

"A significant amount, okay? I mean, not actually a thousand, which is how many you need to have an official library, but . . ." I realize his eyes are getting bigger as I talk. "I really love books."

Why is he staring at me like that? He's standing there with his eyes all glisten-y, one hand on either side of the doorframe above his head. He leans in slightly, never taking his eyes off mine, and suddenly, I feel caged, trapped. His chest looms like a wall blocking my exit. My breath hitches, and instinctively, I want to escape, but as soon as I think it, the urge becomes a fantasy, one where I run and he chases me—and I'm every bit as turned on as I am afraid of what he'll do if he catches me. When he catches me, because there's no way I could outrun him.

The reality is I'd never get past him. He could wrap me up and restrain me with one arm. And then what? My heart pounds like he's already chased me into this room. Like I'm already caught.

He pushes off the doorframe as if my depraved thoughts weren't being broadcast by my body's reactions. "Put it on your punch list, and I'll see what I can come up with. It won't look like you've envisioned it, but I can maybe get you a few extra shelves. Let's go see if I missed any special requests anywhere else."

I step past him into the hallway, and holy shit are my panties soaked. But he is clearly not attracted to me, which is good since we apparently have a non-fraternization policy. Not that he would fraternize with me even if we didn't work together.

He probably goes for women with long legs, dark hair, and sharp fingernails, who've never feared a consequence in their lives, the whole danger-babe vibe.

Truth be told, I bet we're attracted to the same type of women, except he wants to fuck them and I want to be them—girls who don't settle in one place long enough to fill bookshelves. But I'm an overflowing bookshelf kind of girl.

I used to be a wild child who believed I'd grow up to be a wandering free spirit. But then I bought one too many books and found out what health insurance costs, and just like that, I became a girl who needed security and stability. But still needed to get the hell out of her hometown. I did that much, and I did it on my own. No guy tied me there and no guy rescued me from it.

I've got freedom; it's just a different kind than I envisioned growing up.

"You could've chosen different paint colors," Vaughn says as I'm checking out the guest bathroom. "You didn't have to go with the basic beige in every room."

"I know."

"Okay. It just seems like someone who wants custom bookshelves might also want custom paint colors."

"Oh, I do, but not any of the colors we offer. I'm going to paint it myself. And put up some wallpaper."

"Of course, you are."

"What does that mean?"

"We have a dozen colors to choose from. You don't like any of them?"

"I like them fine, but they're not what I want."

"If you'd bought the paint and dropped it off, we could've put it on the walls for you. We had to paint them anyway."

"I didn't even think about that. But I only want certain walls painted."

"Because some are going to be wallpapered."

"Right." I check the last drawer in the vanity and smile at the auto-close feature. Little wild-child Landry would've found drawers that closed by themselves fascinating.

We finish walking the apartment, and I have no complaints in the primary bedroom or bathroom. Before we turn out the lights to go up to the roof, Vaughn says, "Hey, if you buy the paint, leave it in the right rooms, and put sticky notes on the walls you want covered, we'll take care of it before you move in. We don't have that much going on this week."

I thought I'd fully recovered from the lust-fest he'd inspired in my future library, but hearing this incredibly nice offer in his same sexy voice sets that vortex of heat churning in my core again. It's a good thing we're headed up to the roof to hash out what we do and don't know about our new employer. The roof is neutral territory.

Besides, who gets turned on talking about work?

Vaughn

I SWIPE MY CARD on the reader next to the roof access door, and hold it open for Landry to walk through ahead of me. The stairwell is dimly lit, which only makes the silhouette of her ass moving in that black skirt even sexier as she goes up the concrete steps. If I were a more decent man, I'd lift my gaze. *Bullshit. Any straight man with a pulse would be staring at her ass right now.*

There's a second locked door at the top of the stairs, so I reach around her and swipe my card again. "They didn't skimp on security at this place," I say with a laugh, trying to keep the mood light.

"For what we're charging in rent, we better have something extra to offer. Most of the properties around us have twenty-four-hour concierge services. At the white tower on the corner, they offer dog-walking and refueling." She sits in one of the foldable chairs I've set up for us.

The door slams behind me. "How do you refuel a dog?" I flip open the cooler, take a cold bottle, and pop the cap off before I hand it to her.

"Thanks," she says, not bothering to laugh at my lame joke. "If a tenant needs gas in their car, someone will literally come get their keys, go fill up their tank, and bring the keys back to them." She takes a long pull from the bottle, not the dainty first sip I was expecting. "You know, for when you're too exhausted to endure the grueling task of putting gas in your own car."

"I want to punch every pretentious asshole who's ever used that service."

"I'd like to think it's mostly their older tenants who use it, but we both know it's probably the youngest, most able-bodied ones who take advantage of it the most." She lifts her feet out of her heels and pulls her legs up under her. I lean forward in case the chair topples with all that squirming around she's doing, but she doesn't need saving.

Her toenails are painted neon yellow, which is jarring against the rest of her professional façade.

"Interesting nail polish color." I'm legitimately pissed off, thinking about those little shitheads on the corner, having someone else fuel up their cars. I hate the kind of people who live in this part of town. *You live here, asshole.*

"Wasn't looking for your expert critique of my pedicure, but thanks." Her smile is defensive and sarcastic. Goddammit, she's even sexier when she's mad. Of course, she is.

"Sorry. I'm having a hard time adjusting to being surrounded by so much entitlement. I was teasing about your nail polish, didn't mean to say it like that."

"Aw, you mean to tell me Vaughn Sawyer doesn't have a trust fund? That's a trust-fund-baby name if I've ever heard one."

"Yeah, you solved the mystery. I only work because I'm too proud to cash it in."

Her smile softens. "You probably would be."

"What about you?"

"I'm cashing mine in as soon as I turn twenty-six. I can't access it until then."

"How old are you now?"

"I'll be twenty-six in a few months."

That's slightly older than I would've guessed. Don't even start rationalizing. Still too young. In too many ways.

"Oh, so you won't be working here long then."

"Nope. I'll barely be unpacked before I'm rolling around naked in my millions."

Did she have to include the word naked? "Well, you can forget about those bookshelves, now that I know you're a short-timer."

"I didn't say I was moving out. I'm just working here long enough to establish that gas refueling perk. You'll still have to deal with me." She takes another drink of her beer, pressing the mouth of the bottle against her plump bottom lip as she tips it back and swallows. "Every time my tank's empty."

"You probably wouldn't let a man pump your gas unless your legs were broken."

"Two broken legs would make it hard to drive."

"I'm sure you'd find a way." I lower my empty into the cooler and open a second. "What'd you do at your last property, Landry Channing? That's definitely a trust-fund-baby name, by the way."

"In some alternate, luckier universe, maybe I'm a trust-fund-baby. I was the assistant manager. What'd you do at your last property?"

"Same as here, maintenance."

"Why'd you leave to come to The Nouveau?"

"I didn't. I left to go to bootcamp. Ten years ago."

"How old are you?"

I smile at her before I answer. Saying it out loud will bring a barrier down between us, and maybe that's a good thing. "Thirty-five."

"My guess was close. I figured around thirty-one, thirty-two. How old did you think I was?"

"My guess was close, too."

"So, you just got out of the military?"

"Two years ago. I'm a licensed electrician, but it turns out I don't like doing the same thing all day."

"Or did you recently get a divorce, so you needed a place to live and figured why not go back to doing property maintenance, especially at a place that offers a free apartment with the job?"

Wow, she spun that scenario up in no time. "You'd make a quick detective. Not a good one, but quick. What I told you was the whole truth. I was bored, wanted a job where I wasn't doing the same thing, day in and day out, and didn't have to drive all over the city to do it. The free apartment didn't hurt."

She picks at the label on her beer. "Okay. But how long ago was your divorce?"

I laugh. Apparently, when she wants an answer, she doesn't give up. "Five years. Are you happy now?" *Why does she care if I'm divorced, or for how long?*

"Me, too."

"You, too, what?"

"I got divorced five years ago, too."

"When you were twenty?"

"Almost twenty-one. We got married at eighteen."

"Young love."

"Small town. Very, very small town."

"Any kids?"

"Ah, see, that's the popular assumption. I must've been pregnant to have gotten married so young, right? Nope, just under a lot of pressure. I agreed to get married, but not to give up on college. And there was no way I was having kids before I got my degree. I got the divorce with no kids, and then I finished the degree."

"Your parents must've been proud of that much, at least."

"You'd think, but they were much prouder of the getting married part."

"Really? I assumed the pressure to get married was probably from the guy, not your parents."

"It was from everyone, everywhere, all at once. What about you?" she asks with her eyes fixed on me like she needs to see my face when I answer. "Kids?"

"Nope. She never wanted any, and I'd never thought about it much either way, so I was fine with her choice."

"Until you weren't?"

"No, that had nothing to do with why we got divorced. I still have no idea if I want kids or not."

"Me either."

Our eyes lock, and for a moment, there's a vulnerability in hers, but she blinks it away as quickly as I noticed it.

"So, what exactly were you told when you took this job?" she asks.

Part of me wants to bring the conversation back to personal topics, but I know Landry won't let me. I also know I shouldn't.

We recount our interviews for each other, and quickly determine we were both pretty much given a matching spiel: recent major renovations, unexpected staff upheaval, low tenant turnover, great location, free apartment, solid benefits . . . same dog and pony show that left us both questioning what was being left out, but we jumped at the chances anyway.

"They sure didn't mention anything about Lolita, the snake." Landry laughs, swirling the last few inches of beer left in her bottle. "I guess I don't need to tell you I'm slightly terrified of snakes."

"Never would've guessed. You seemed so at ease when Lolita came slithering through the office."

She laughs. "Sorry for invading your personal space like that. I can't believe Carina just loved on that thing like it was a puppy."

"She is a pretty snake."

"Those two words don't even belong in the same sentence."

"You should probably get some desensitivity training. I bet you're going to encounter Lolita pretty often. I don't get the impression Vonnie worries a whole lot about other people's reactions to much of anything."

"Oh, she definitely doesn't care how I feel about her snake." She downs the rest of her beer, flips open the lid to the cooler, slides her empty into the ice, and helps herself to another bottle. I like that she didn't ask or wait for me to offer. "But she's very interested in your reaction to her."

She twists the cap off her fresh beer instead of asking me to do it. That impresses me more than it should. Of course, she's capable of twisting a damn cap off a bottle. It's just that she's got a fragile look about her—at first glance, anyway. But she's not, and I'm even more intrigued than I was initially. "I've always liked snakes."

"I meant herself, not her snake, Vaughn. That woman wanted to see how you'd react to *her*."

"Oh. Yeah. She's not exactly discreet. But she couldn't have been a burlesque star if she was shy."

"An aging stripper with a wandering pet snake on day one." She shakes her head. "Can't wait to see what tomorrow brings."

"Burlesque isn't exactly stripping," I say. "There's more to the performance than dancers in a strip club."

"I've never been to a burlesque show."

"How many strip clubs have you been to?" I said it to tease her, but the way her eyes narrow over her upturned bottle tells me it didn't land well. Shit. I didn't mean to offend her. Maybe she stripped at some point. I wouldn't judge her for that, but I can't imagine Landry stripping. *Liar. You're imagining it right now. Fuck.*

I shake my head to dislodge the images, and immediately wave my hand in front of my face like I'm trying to brush away a mosquito. It's Houston. Bugs are everywhere. Maybe she didn't even notice. Her eyes are still on me though.

"I've been to a strip club." She takes another swig from her bottle. "I have a friend who danced for a while."

A friend, huh? Leave it alone. It's none of your business.

"I thought about it," she volunteers as if she can read my thoughts. "She was making good money. Easy money. Quick money. But I don't have what it takes."

My eyes scan her body before I can stop them. She laughs, makes no attempt to pretend she didn't notice.

"I didn't mean I didn't have what it takes physically. I had no problem with her doing it; hell, I admired her in some ways. But it wasn't for me, so I kept waiting tables in a cheap steakhouse for a fraction of the cash she was raking in."

"Did you go with your ex?"

"No. I went with friends, people I knew from college who were more open-minded than my uptight ex-husband."

"What's he doing now?"

"Remarried. Has two kids already. Living in our hometown, less than a mile from his parents, like a good son."

"And you ran away."

"As fast as I could." She tips her bottle back again. "How about your ex? What's she up to these days?"

"Last I heard she was living in Miami. She likes the beach. And the bars."

"Ah. Got it. You married the party girl who wasn't ready to settle down."

"Something like that." I swipe at a real mosquito. "Mostly, she just didn't want to be a military wife anymore."

"But you liked being in the military?"

"No, I was over it by then, too. But I had a few years left, and she couldn't wait. We were pretty much done, anyway. Neither one of us fought it."

I don't know what's happening here because I never talk about this stuff. I asked Landry to come up here to talk about work, yet somehow, we've shared more personal shit than anything else. She is way too damn easy to talk to. And I need to shut the fuck up.

"I have friends whose husbands enlisted. That life wouldn't have been for me either."

"Probably not. So, did anything else interesting happen on your first day?"

"Not really. I fielded a lot of complaints about the gate on the garage being broken so often. One guy wants a new dishwasher because we advertise quiet appliances, and his is too loud. A woman stopped by the office to let me know she finds the carpet in the hallway on her floor tacky."

"Dishwasher guy is on the fourth floor, right? Tall, curly hair, wears scrubs?"

"Yeah, that's him. Is he a doctor?"

"I think he's a physical therapist or something. I've looked at his dishwasher already. It's fine. I suggested he invest in some earplugs."

"You did not say that to him."

"Don't worry, I said it with a smile. Sort of." I shrug.

"Is this your first luxury property, Vaughn? You have to suck it up sometimes and be nice to people, whether you like them or not. The tenants here are going to have high expectations, and sometimes they might seem ridiculous, but we can't dismiss them like that."

"He was fine." *Is she seriously trying to school me on how to deal with people? I was navigating foreign lands while she was still learning to solve for x.*

"Just be nice, okay?"

"I am nice."

"You might need to polish up your version of nice."

"Hey, you want those bookshelves or not?"

"Damn, my bookshelves are conditional now? What else do I have to do to keep you on the job?"

Don't respond to that. Not even jokingly. Especially not jokingly.

Landry

SITTING IN A FOLDING chair, pulling beers from a cooler feels like old times. The view's better here, and Vaughn buys better beer, but the familiarity has me letting down my guard way more than I should. Why the hell did I tell him I'd been married and divorced? Or to a strip club?

Fine, I know why I told him about the strip club, and I need to stop telling him things for that reason most of all. It's been a long time since I've wanted to say something to a guy just to see his reaction, to see if he'll be shocked or turned on, or both.

Most men show exactly what they're thinking. So easy to read. Vaughn's more careful. Like I usually am. Hell, if his eyes hadn't done that rapid auto-scan of my body at the mention of strippers, I wouldn't even be sure he'd noticed I had boobs.

Not that I'd wanted him to notice. Okay, I definitely wanted him to notice. I'm not sure if I want him to act on it, though, but I do love letting it play out in my head. At least I know he sees me as an option, whether it'll lead to anything or not. These are dangerous thoughts that I should not be entertaining at all. I probably shouldn't drink the rest of this beer either. I've barely eaten anything today. "What do you think the odds are that we could get pizza delivered up here?"

He pulls his phone from his pocket and taps on the screen.

"Are you ordering?"

"It's the only way I know to get a definitive answer to your question. What toppings do you want?"

"Fresh mozzarella, spinach, artichoke hearts, and prosciutto."

"Where the hell do you think I'm ordering this pizza from? Rome?"

"Luna's has those toppings. They're right down the street. I'm sure they deliver here."

His sigh gives way to a grin. "Fine. City girl."

"Hey, I didn't just get here, you know."

"How long have you been in Houston?" He sets his phone on the overturned plastic bucket he's had his feet propped on.

"Three years. What'd you tell them for delivery instructions?"

"To knock on the roof access door at the end of the hallway on the eighth floor."

"Will we hear them?" The HVAC units are up here. They're not quiet.

"Maybe." His eyes shine in the dusk. It'll be dark soon, but for now, I can still see the way he looks at me. For the first time, I think maybe he's having the same types of thoughts about me as I am about him. "The security camera will send me an alert before they even get to the door, though."

"Are you supposed to have the security feed on your phone?" His stare is unreadable again. But then his sly grin returns. He doesn't answer my question, though.

I think I know the answer.

But for some reason, I kind of like knowing he can see what goes on in our hallway. I'd sooner have my fingernails ripped off with pliers than admit it out loud, but it makes me feel safer. *He makes me feel safe.* Oh, fuck, I should not have asked him to order a pizza. I should be headed for a drive-through burger on my way home right now.

Before I know it, I've finished the rest of the beer I'd intended to save until after I'd eaten something, and opened another one. I've lost track of my intentions, gotten caught up listening to one of Vaughn's stories about another interesting tenant I haven't met yet.

If the delivery driver had followed instructions and simply knocked, we might not have heard him, but since he pounds on the door like a lunatic two seconds after the camera alert buzzes Vaughn's phone, there's no way we could miss him.

His timing's good. I need food on my stomach as soon as possible. "How much do I owe you?" I ask.

Vaughn sets the pizza box on the bucket, and flips open the lid. It smells like cheesy, garlicky heaven. "You don't owe me anything."

"No, seriously. It was my idea to order. I can at least pay for my half of it."

"Who said I'm letting you have half?" He hands me a slice, and I need to shove it in my face immediately, before I flirt back with him. Assuming he's flirting. For all I know, he grins at everybody like that when he talks to them. I don't actually know him. And I have a slight buzz, so my interpretations can't be trusted right now.

I might not even be attracted to him when I'm fully sober again. *Whatever. You were attracted to him long before you drank the first sip.*

The pizza's good, and Vaughn's stories keep getting better. He's only been here a week, but already, he's had so many funny interactions with tenants. It sounds like working here is going to be a wild ride. *Do not look at his crotch when you think that. Look away from his crotch!*

My hand slides into the cooler. Plunging a body part into ice seems like a good idea right now. I feel around but every bottle top is bare. We drank them all? It's completely dark now, and I have no idea what time it is, but I definitely need to go. "I'll help you take this stuff inside."

"Don't worry about it. I've got it." He stands, but freezes like a statue. "Shit, you don't live here yet."

"Four more days," I say, wistfully. I'd spin around with my arms outstretched again if I didn't fear falling on my ass. My buzz has faded, but it's been my experience that beer, pizza, and dizziness don't play well together.

"You can't drive home," he says.

"Of course, I can. I'm fine."

"Bullshit. You can stay at my place and sneak out early in the morning."

My mouth goes dry. I can't . . . I mean . . . there's no way. Right?

"That's not happening." I loop my purse over my shoulder, but Vaughn grabs the strap before I can take a step.

"You're staying with me."

His voice is so deep and authoritative, and his grip on my purse strap is tight. And I'm nodding. Why am I nodding? *Stop nodding!*

He picks up the pizza box and the bucket, but leaves the cooler. "I'll get that tomorrow. Come on."

What choice do I have at this point? I already nodded! I'll crash on his couch, and slink out to make my cross-town commute before the sun comes up. Ugh. I really should've thought this through better.

When he opens his front door, it becomes immediately apparent my plans are about to change again. "Vaughn, where's you couch?" I ask.

"On back order."

"Oh." *Oh, shit.*

I breathe a sigh of relief, remembering we both have a two-bedroom unit. "I hope the room service is decent in this place. I'll be ringing for coffee from your guest bed as soon as I wake up in the morning." I turn to smile at him, but he's looking at me like he doesn't realize I'm joking.

"I don't have one of those."

"One of what? A coffee maker?"

"A guest bed."

I head down his hallway as if I didn't hear that. He's just messing with me. Maybe I won't find a bed, but a futon, or his old couch—I'm sure I'll find something in his guest room. And I do.

But I can't sleep on a treadmill, or a weight set. "We have a gym onsite. Why do you need this stuff in your apartment?"

"Because if I use the onsite gym, tenants will hound me while I'm trying to work out."

"Yeah, they probably would. Okay, so do you at least have extra blankets so I can make a pallet on the floor?"

"You're not sleeping on the damn floor, Landry. You can sleep in my bed."

That's so sweet, but I can't let him sleep on the floor. He rounds the corner into his bedroom. "I've got extra toothbrushes. I'll give you a tee shirt to sleep in."

"Are these extra toothbrushes unused?" I ask, playfully, as I trail him into his room.

He tosses a shirt from his dresser toward me. "Brand new, princess."

I laugh. This shirt's not new. It's well-worn and buttery soft, and if I held it up to my nose, I know it would smell like him, like sage, brown sugar, and all the warm spices mixed together. Thanksgiving. That's what it is. He smells like Thanksgiving dinner. And his hair looks windblown like the first cold front just hit. It's almost summer, but he's the walking embodiment of fall. My favorite season. I bet he looks good in a cap and a flannel. *Stop that.*

He disappears into his bathroom to brush his teeth before me. When he comes back, he's shirtless, but he's wearing a pair of basketball shorts. His bare chest and upper arms reveal more tattoos, and my fingertips prickle when I think about how it would feel to trace them on his skin—another thought I need to stop having immediately.

"Thanks, Vaughn. I appreciate it." I hold up his shirt and shrug, not knowing what else to say. "You really don't have to do this."

"Oh, I absolutely have to loan you a shirt. I wouldn't trust myself in the same bed with you if you were naked." He winks.

"Same bed? No way." He better wipe that grin off his face right now. "We are not sleeping in the same bed."

"I only have the one. How else did you see this playing out?"

"I thought you were offering to sleep on the floor."

He throws his head back when he laughs. So dramatic. "Oh, you are a princess, aren't you? I'm offering you one side of the bed, sweetheart, not the whole thing."

"We can't sleep together. I'm your boss!"

"You are most definitely *not* my boss."

"I most definitely am."

"Did someone tell you that in your interview?"

"No one had to tell me. That's how it goes. I'm the property manager, Vaughn. I'm everyone's boss."

His head hinges back on his neck again, and his laughter rolls out like a wave. "Right. You need to brush your damn teeth and put that shirt on so I can turn out the light. You've got to get up ridiculously early tomorrow."

I clench his shirt and twist like I'm wringing water out of it. "I'll sleep on the floor."

"I really don't have any extra blankets. Not even sheets."

"Yes, you do. Everybody has extra sheets and blankets." I storm into the bathroom to brush my teeth, pee, and put on his velvety soft shirt. Before I come out, I fold my clothes neatly with my bra tucked safely between my skirt and shirt, as if him seeing my bra would be the biggest scandal of this evening. I'd have left it on if I could sleep in one but I can't.

Not that it will matter if I'm wearing a bra or not. All that sexual attraction I felt on the roof is gone. Zip. Zilch. Nada. Smug jerk. I have a car. I could just drive myself home. And I still might.

After setting my clothes on his dresser, I place my shoes neatly on the floor in front of it, and move to his closet to find what I need for my makeshift bed. His top shelves have boxes, no blankets. There are none on his lower shelves either. He sits with his back against the headboard, watching me search.

"Are they in the linen closet?" I ask.

He shrugs. "You're not going to believe me, anyway, so you may as well go look."

I stomp back into the bathroom and fling open the cabinet doors. No blankets. I check the hall closet. Nothing. "You were in the freaking military! You have to have a sleeping bag somewhere."

"If you find one, you're welcome to use it." He turns out the lamp, fluffs up his pillow, and snuggles in like he's about to sail off to dreamland.

"Who doesn't have a sleeping bag? Everybody has a sleeping bag!"

"Like I said, if you find one, it's all yours."

How can he have no extra sheets or blankets? That's ridiculous. Who lives like that?

I flip off the hall light and walk back into his room, where I turn on the overhead light so I can see to get my clothes.

Vaugh sits up, shielding his eyes with his hand. "What the hell are you doing now?"

"Putting my clothes back on so I can go home."

"Oh, no you're not."

"Oh, yes I am." I grab my clothes and hold them against my chest as I head for his bathroom to change.

Before I take a second step, his arms are around my waist and he's lifting me off the ground, carrying me toward his bed. I flail and kick, but his grip is like a vise. "Put me down!"

"I'm about to." He drops me onto his bed, and snatches my clothes away. My bra goes flying. "Crawl your ass under the covers and go to sleep." I wiggle under the covers, but only because his t-shirt is twisted up around my waist now.

As soon as I have the shirt straightened and pulled back down below my hips, I flay the comforter aside, and swing my legs over the edge of the bed. He drops my shirt and skirt, and grabs my ankles before my feet reach the floor. With my legs immobilized in his tight grip, he spins me back onto the mattress before he drops them. "Stop it, Landry. You're staying in this bed."

"You can't hold me hostage!"

"You're not a hostage. You're a guest. Goodnight."

The moment he starts to climb back in on his side of the bed, I make a run for it, grabbing my clothes from the floor as I go.

Half a second before I reach his bedroom door, he slams it and splays his palm flat against it. "You are not driving yourself home."

"Fine. Then you can drive me home."

"Nope. I've been drinking, too. And I'm tired."

"I'll get a ride."

"It's your money. Spend it however you want." His hand remains on the door. "But your car key stays with me. You can have it back tomorrow."

"I need my keys to get into my apartment."

"Not your car key, you don't."

"You are infuriating."

"Right back at ya, babe." His other arm comes around to cage me, both his hands now holding the door closed as his chest grazes my back. "If I'd known you were going to act like this after a few beers, I wouldn't have offered you the first one."

"I am a grown-ass woman. I can handle a few beers. I'm acting this way because you're acting like a Neanderthal!"

"For wanting to keep you safe? You're being a brat. You need your ass spanked." His body goes rigid, and he sucks in a breath, like he didn't mean to say that.

In sharp contrast, my body starts to melt. Why? What just happened? It's all I can do to hold myself steady between his arms. The heat coming off his chest feels like his skin just turned to magma. Who does he think he is, talking to me like that? He can't say something like that to me. And I'd tell him so, if I could remember how to speak.

His muscles relax enough for his body to grant a few inches of space between us, but his hands stay on the door. "Just stay here, Landry. I'm exhausted. If you use a ride app, I'll lie awake and worry until you text to let me know you made it home safe, which I'm sure you'd forget to do. We both need sleep. I have a perfectly comfortable bed, big enough that we never even have to touch. Please, make this easy."

"Fine." Not like I could drive now, anyway. My whole body is shaking on the inside, and it's probably only a matter of seconds before the tremors make their way to the surface. I actually need to lie down as soon as possible. "No touching."

"Deal." His voice is raspy. Whatever just spiked between us needs to never rear its head again. We both need sleep, like he said. Bodies act weird when they're exhausted.

He moves away to let me step freely back into the room. I don't bother refolding my clothes, just drop them on the floor, and crawl into the far side of the bed, keeping my back to him. The mattress dips under his weight. "Goodnight, Landry."

"Night."

My body feels like it's plugged into an electrical outlet the moment the room falls into darkness. The door is still shut, making the space feel too private, too cozy for comfort. All I can do is lie here with my thoughts spinning and nerves zinging. Everything would've been fine if he'd just had extra sheets and blankets like a normal person.

"What if sex makes things messy?" *What the actual fuck? Why did I say that out loud?* I think he's already asleep. Maybe he didn't hear it.

"What?"

Great. He's a light sleeper. "It just really bothers me that you only have one set of sheets."

"Oh, you meant an actual physical mess."

"Yeah, I mean, if you're having sex and the sheets get totally wrecked, what do you do? You don't have an extra set to swap out so you can sleep."

"Nobody gets up and changes their damn sheets because sex got messy. You just roll over and go to sleep."

"Oh, my God. Tell me you're not that guy."

"What guy?"

"The one who does what you just said."

"How messy do you make the sheets?"

Is it my imagination or is he radiating volcanic heat again all of a sudden? This bed just got hot. "Never mind. I'm sorry I woke you up. Go back to sleep."

"Huh," he says in the dark. When his body shifts into a new position, I swear I hear him murmur, "fuuuuck me."

I try to lie still, I swear, but I can't get comfortable. His mattress is too luxurious. This level of comfort makes me uncomfortable. And who knows how often he washes these sheets? He clearly thinks it's fine to sleep on them in any condition. I reach down and feel across the sheet under my body. It's smooth. What if it hadn't been? What if my hand had found a stiff spot? Oh, my God. That's so gross. Now, I'm never going to be able to fall asleep.

"Stop fidgeting and go to sleep."

Oh, damn. His sleepy mad voice is even sexier than his wide-awake mad voice. "I'm trying. I can't." I whisper, like the volume of my voice makes a difference at this point.

He rolls over to face me, and without saying a word, he grabs my inner thigh and pulls my leg against his body. "Wh-what are you doing?"

"Putting you to sleep, princess."

I should stop him. But his hand is so warm over my panties, and then his fingers slide the satin down until his rough skin is rubbing over the smoothness of mine. When I open my mouth to say we shouldn't, all that comes out is a moan—a prolonged moan that should leave me feeling ashamed, but his finger strokes through my wetness, dragging my arousal up to my clit, and circling it with the most perfect pressure anyone has ever applied with no instruction at all from me. He touches me like he already knows my body, like he's done this a thousand times before.

When his finger slides back down and enters my pussy, the sound I make is higher pitched and clipped. He moans at that, and I know we're not stopping until I've wrecked his only sheets.

He inserts a second finger, and immediately, my second leg spreads wide for him. *Just don't kiss me. As long as you don't kiss me—* His breath is warm and still minty from his toothpaste. His lips are soft and his tongue is touching mine before I realize it's too late for boundaries; he's already kissing me. And I'm kissing him back.

His mouth abruptly separates from mine. Maybe kissing was against his rules, too? This is good. At least one of us is thinking clearly.

But when he takes his fingers away from my pussy, my hips lift to chase them, and the mewling sound that leaves my mouth makes me want to bury my face in a pillow. His hand is back on my body—for as long as it takes to pull his t-shirt over my head. My hair catches in it for a moment, but he frees it with one smooth wrist-flick, and then it's on the floor with my clothes.

The room is still dark, but my eyes have adjusted enough that I can see him drinking in my nakedness for a few seconds before his hand follows the path of his gaze across my chest.

I thought he was just going to get me off, and maybe I'd return the favor, and then we'd both go to sleep, and disregard this whole encounter in the light of day, but now . . . now, I know this is about to be more.

If this is a mistake, it won't be my first.

As hard as my brain is working to infuse logic here, it's completely overpowered by his touch. His hand on my skin radiates warmth like he's laying a dozen hands on me at once, and he's kissing me again.

When his mouth leaves mine and peppers kisses across my neck and chest, pausing to suck on my hardened nipple before trailing licks and nibbles down my stomach, the scorching heat of his lips and tongue leaves a chill in its wake, a shiver that can only be quelled by his hot hand still roving over my body.

That same hand makes quick work of removing my panties as easily as he stripped his shirt from me.

When his head is positioned between my spread legs, and his mouth savors the first taste of what his fingers have coaxed from my pussy, both his hands reach up to roam over my body, warming and relaxing me until all the tension in my body releases, rendering me languid and complicit in whatever these walls are about to witness.

If his tongue is still licking and probing me like this when my alarm goes off, the lost sleep will be a fair casualty. I'll suffer any consequences tomorrow as long as he doesn't stop tonight.

His comforter is bunched at the foot of the bed where he's kicked it down and out of the way, and I don't miss the cover at all. Lying fully exposed to him feels like the right way to do this. *Give the man room to work.*

My legs begin to shake at the same instant my smaller muscles start to quake, and I simultaneously want to prolong the ecstasy and to let it happen all at once, to come faster and harder than I ever have.

The latter option wins out, and when he rises up onto his hands and positions his body over mine, he's breathing nearly as hard as I am.

And that moan when the tip's in is not a solo performance; it's a fucking duet.

Vaughn

SHE TASTES AS SWEET as she looks, and feels better than both combined. And the sounds she's making are straight out of my fantasies. She's dangerous, but I couldn't stop now if the building was on fire. *This pussy is fire.*

"You like that?" I rise up with one hand pressed into the mattress and the other resting between her ribs and roll my hips forward until my cock is buried balls-deep in her perfect little snatch. Her juices are everywhere, and she's so fucking hot. She doesn't answer my question, not with words.

But, damn. That little yelp before the moan? Yeah, I'm going to need to hear that again. Pulling my hips so soon is torture because I want to stay fully sheathed in this tight cunt every bit as much as I want to hear that sound leave her beautiful mouth again. She repeats it when my hips rock forward, and I hit the same spot again. Her body tenses and relaxes like a reflex.

If I could, I'd chase this reaction from her all night long, but I can already feel my control slipping. I'm not going to last. On my next thrust, she rolls her hips up to meet mine, matching my rhythm.

My eyes have adjusted to the dark, enabling me to see that she's staring up at me, watching me fuck her. She extends one leg, hooks her ankle behind mine, and wraps her other leg around my lower back, squeezing to pull me deeper into her. The soft skin of her inner legs feels so fucking good rubbing against my leg and my back, and her slick pussy's drawing me in. Trying to hold on is no use; my dick lurches and my hips jerk.

I roll onto my back and wait for regret to consume me as my breathing steadies. But the sweet scent of her shampoo or perfume or whatever I've been catching whiffs off all night fills the room, and I don't regret a single moment.

The sun will come up and usher in all the regret, no matter how hard I try to pretend it's not there, but for now, it's nowhere to be found. When I roll toward her, she moves her face to mine, and I'm not sure who initiates the kiss, but I'm not going to be the one to end it.

The kiss fades, and I stroke her cheek with the back of my hand, pausing when I realize her face feels damp. "Tell me that's sweat and not tears," I whisper in the dark.

"Sometimes, my eyes leak during sex." Her voice is soft. "It's just a form of release, not actual crying, not from sadness or pain or anything. Don't be freaked out, okay? I'm fine. I promise."

God, she sounds so sweet, completely unguarded and vulnerable right now, and I know the moment she realizes it, her defenses will go back up.

I believe her about the tears being a release, but I don't think she's fine. Not really. I may have just met her, but I know her. *Fuuuuck me. Maybe my next life will be less complicated.*

"I think you wrecked my sheets."

"I think we both knew that was going to happen as soon as you put your hand on my leg." Her voice is already stronger. "I can't believe you don't even have a sleeping bag."

"It's under the bed."

"You jerk."

"You're not the first woman to call me that." I kiss her softly before I climb over her and head for the bathroom, dragging the comforter off the bed as I go. She clutches at it, but she's too late. "Stay put."

"Don't tell me what to do."

She's still lying naked and beautiful on my soaked sheets when I come back with a warm cloth. She reaches her hand to take it from me. "I've got it," I say. Her knees draw together as soon as I offer. "Open your legs for me."

"I can do it myself."

"You can, but you shouldn't have to. Open your legs." Her thighs part. The way she obeys me like that makes me want to go for round two, but we've probably only got a few hours of sleep ahead of us as it is. I'd say the hell with sleep altogether if I was only worried about me, but she has to drive home and back again before work.

She shivers when the cloth meets her tender skin. When I stop, she sits up and slips past me. I turn and watch her silhouetted curves disappear into the bathroom before I strip the fitted sheet off the mattress and toss it into the hamper along with the washcloth.

When it's fully unzipped, the sleeping bag almost covers the surface of the mattress. It makes a soft pad, anyway, and it's dry. I'm pulling the top sheet and comforter over it when Landry comes back from the bathroom. I fold it open for her, and she doesn't say a word, just stumbles forward and crawls into my bed with no argument.

She's asleep within minutes, her hair splayed across the pillow and her legs encroaching on my side. I slide closer to the edge and let her have the extra space, close my eyes, and try to ignore the memories clawing to make comparisons to the past. All my defense mechanisms are gearing up. I slow my breathing, forcing longer exhales than inhales.

Landry

I REACH FOR MY phone to shut off my alarm, but my hand doesn't land on my bedside table. There's nothing there. It's still dark outside. Why is my bed so fluffy? *Oh, fuck.*

Last night comes rushing back like a tidal wave, pinning me to the mattress. Or, more accurately, to Vaughn's sleeping bag on top of his mattress. I squeeze my eyes shut and pretend it was all a dream, but when I open them again, I'm still in his apartment. And his alarm is still going off. I lunge for the nightstand on his side of the bed and slap at the screen until it shuts up.

Only one nightstand. Of course. One set of sheets, one blanket, one of everything . . .

There's a light on at the end of the hall. In the kitchen? My gaze is captured by the outline of his body. It's a frontal view; he's coming back to his room. No basketball shorts, just boxer briefs that hug his toned body. It shouldn't be a big deal at this point; I've seen him in less.

No, you've only felt him in less. It was dark. You couldn't see that final, tight section of lower abs, the trail of dark curls that leads down, down . . .

Maybe I should've let my hands wander over his body a little more last night, because I sure can't do it now. Or ever again.

"I made you coffee for the road. It's in the black tumbler on the counter. I don't have any milk or anything for it, but I left room in case you wanted to grab some creamer from the office on your way out."

"Thanks. I'll um, just get dressed, and get out of here."

"Getting dressed first is probably a good idea."

He turns the lamp on, and I immediately want him to turn it back off. He looks way too good to have just rolled out of bed. That's not fair. I probably look like a damn swamp monster. I turn and search the floor for my scattered clothes, but I spot them folded neatly and set back on the end of his dresser.

"How long have you been awake?" I ask.

"Not long."

I think he's lying. He probably wants me to get the hell out of here so he can go back to sleep.

Staring at myself in his bathroom mirror, I make another pass over my face with a cool washcloth. So, second day on the job, and the worst mistake I've made so far is I fucked one of my employees last night. Totally minor. No big deal at all.

And now I have to make the walk of shame out of the building with raccoon eyes, frizzy sex hair twisted up in a claw clip, and wearing yesterday's wrinkled clothes. And hope no tenants catch me. Yeah, I'm drinking that coffee black because there is no way I can risk stopping in the office.

I take a deep breath, and walk out of his bathroom. He's not in the bedroom, which feels like a kindness if I'm being honest. When I step into the hallway, I hear the hum of his treadmill. Glancing into the room as I pass, I give him a quick wave. His shorts are back on, and I'm sure he notices when my eyes drop to check.

"Drive safe," he says.

"Thanks." I pull my eyes up to meet his. "And thanks for the coffee. And for last night. I mean, the pizza. And the beer." Why is my face getting hot? I don't have to see it to know I'm blushing.

He smiles without missing a step. "You're welcome." There's a sound, like maybe he's about to say more, so I pause, but he looks down at the controls and increases his incline without another word.

"Have a good day," I say before I resume my exit.

"You, too." He jerks his chin up quickly, but doesn't make eye contact.

I grab the coffee from his counter and take a gulp as I let myself out. This is the strongest coffee I've ever tasted. I hate black coffee to begin with, but this tastes like poison. How the hell does he drink it?

My breath leaves my body like air being let out of a balloon when I finally make it to my car in the parking garage. Mission accomplished.

As soon as I shift into reverse and start to roll back out of my parking spot, the motion sensors flash and beep at me, indicating there is something at my right rear bumper. I hit the brakes and check my mirrors.

It's still dark out, and the scream that leaves my mouth when a figure steps up to my passenger-side door could wake the dead. He's not a large man. Or a young one. The small, gray-haired man smiling in at me knocks on the window and waves. I wave back tentatively, but I don't put the car in park, or roll down the window.

What does he want? He looks harmless, but why would a harmless old man be wandering through the parking garage at this hour? He's wearing a fedora, for fuck's sake. Where is he going?

I shrug at him, and he motions for me to roll down the window. Against my better judgment, which I thought only left me temporarily last night, I roll down the window and put the car in park. "Can I help you?"

"You're the new manager, aren't you?"

"I am, yes. I'm Landry Channing."

"I knew it. I'm sorry to have startled you, but they said you were a young, pretty blonde, and when I saw you, I just knew. It's a pleasure to meet you, Miss Channing." He tips his hat, and I'm not sure if that's adorable or a warning sign. "I'm Autry McDaniel. I've lived here since the building first opened, so if you need anything or have any questions, you feel free to give me a call."

He hands me a business card, but when I look at it, there's no company name or position listed; it's just his name and phone number in black ink on a silver background, but there's a top hat tilted on the M at the beginning of his last name, like a personal logo. Oh, hell. He's definitely adorable.

"Thank you, Mr. McDaniel. I recognize your name. You're one of the first two tenants. You and Vonnie, right?"

"Oh, please don't mention that vile woman to me so early in the morning! I haven't even had my oatmeal."

I stifle a laugh. "I'm sorry. I take it you two aren't close?" As if I don't already know.

"Close? Have you ever seen what happens when oil and water try to get close? They repel each other, just like I'm repelled by that crude woman and her serpent."

"I have to be honest with you," I say. "I'm not a fan of the snake either."

"Which one?"

We lock eyes, and as hard as I try not to, I crack up. Autry McDaniel is a funny man. I like him, even if he did nearly give me a pre-dawn heart attack. He laughs along with me for a few moments, but he stops suddenly. "You didn't work all night, did you?"

"Oh, no. I just, um, uh . . . *Think, dammit. Stop stammering.* "I can't officially move in until this weekend, but I was so tired after work yesterday, I went up to my apartment to take a quick nap and wait for traffic to die down. When I woke up, it was time to drive home and get ready for work again."

"First day jitters can be exhausting." He nods like he understands completely. "You didn't sleep on the hard floor, I hope."

"Oh, no. Vaughn lives right across the hall, and thanks to his sleeping bag, I slept like a baby." *Not technically a lie, although his sleeping bag doesn't really deserve all the credit.*

Autry nods again. "Ah, yes, our new maintenance supervisor. Former military. Good man." The he leans in and says, "You watch yourself around him, young lady."

"You just said he was a good man."

"Sure, I like him just fine. He's a real man's man. But you're a beautiful young woman, and even the best of men can behave less than respectably at times. He's older than you, but still young enough to be stupid."

Wow, early morning misogyny wrapped in a backhanded compliment. This day just keeps getting better. "I'll keep my eye on him."

"I'm more worried about him keeping his eyes on you. But I should let you get going. You be careful on your way this morning."

"I will. It was nice to meet you."

"Lovely to meet you, Landry. Welcome to The Nouveau." He steps away from my car and bows like a ringmaster, which feels appropriate since this place is shaping up to have serious three-ring circus vibes.

Vaughn

I PASS ALL THE minor repair requests to Holden, and then I get busy, picking through our shelving options in storage. Holden's more than capable of handling everything on the service orders, and he's probably tired of having me breathing down his neck all the time, anyway.

There's a lot more in here than I thought. And it's not like we have any tenants waiting on the office conversion for their second bedroom, so nobody's going to miss them if I give them all to Landry. I can probably spare some of the maintenance budget to get trim pieces to finish them out, and make them look a little nicer for her.

A ladder on a rail is not happening, but I guess a few extra shelves isn't really too much for her to ask. Like I said, nobody else is using them.

I'm not doing this just because of what happened between us last night. I already knew I was going to do this for her as soon as I saw the disappointment in her eyes when she realized there'd been a misunderstanding about her request. She was getting these shelves long before we made it up to the roof, before she ever flashed that tipsy smile at me or told me about being married so young or how she felt about her hometown, before she requested those specialty pizza toppings or—"Ow, fuck!"

I step back and free my sleeve from the nail that's snagged it and scratched the hell out of my shoulder in the process. Oh, well. That's one shirt ruined. Who leaves a damn nail in a board and just leans it against the wall like that? The last maintenance man they had here must've been a fucking idiot. *And you're the fucking idiot who just walked right into it.*

The board clatters onto a pile of castaway materials when I toss it in the corner of the room. Somebody needs to get in here and organize this shit. That'll be good busy work for Holden on a slow day. I've done my time with grunt work. He can do his.

Before I know it, I've got a trolley loaded with shelves to be assembled and hung in Landry's *almost library*. I wheel it down the hall to her door, and that's when I realize she kept the key after I let her open her own door last night.

When I walk into the office, she's laughing at something Carina has said. She's wearing a bright blue dress, her long hair falling in waves over her shoulder as her head falls to the side. She looks so carefree, so unlike my first impression of her.

They both stop laughing as soon as they see me, looking suspiciously stunned, like they're equally worried about what I might've overheard, which was nothing, but I'm not going to let them know that. "Wow," I say. "Keeping it professional in the office, I see."

Carina ducks her head sheepishly and turns toward her computer. She definitely thinks I overhead something.

Landry, on the other hand, she's ready to spar. "We've got things under control in the office, but I have a list here for you." She holds up a notepad. "319 needs their air filters changed. 501 says this is her third request to have her shower drain unclogged—"

I snatch the notepad from her hand. "Holden has the air filters for 319, and he's probably already changed them. I'll send him to check on 501's drain. I'm sure she just needs to pull her own hair out of it, but sure, we'll do it for her."

"Um," Carina says, quietly. "I have a feeling 501 probably wants you to come check on her drain, not Holden."

"What is she, some VIP tenant or something?" This place seems to have more than its share of those.

"No. But she thinks you're incredibly hot. Fair warning, she'll probably come to the door wearing a towel. Or lingerie. She has a history."

I laugh. "Well, I'm sure she'll make Holden's day." I shoot him a quick text, and then I send a second, warning him not to even think about touching her, no matter what she's wearing when she opens the door, not even if she initiates, not even if she insists it's okay, not even if she falls and claims to need his help getting up. No touching. Not if he wants to keep his job.

And no, I don't feel like a hypocrite. An employee fucking a tenant is a whole different situation than me and Landry. End of discussion.

It occurs to me that Holden's first thought will be what a great scene that would make for his screenplay. Okay, it might be his second thought, but I know he's going to think about it for too damn long to make the right choice. I haven't even seen the woman who lives in 501, but I've been his age. I text him again and tell him to scratch 501 from his list. I'll take care of that one.

I turn back to Landry. "Anything else?"

"Nope. That's it."

"All right."

"Where are you going?"

"To do my job."

"Okay. I thought maybe you came in here for a reason."

Shit. "Yeah, I need your key."

"Oh, I forgot I still had it" She opens a drawer in her desk and pulls out her purse, but she doesn't even look in it before she says, "I don't have it. It's in the pocket of my skirt from yesterday."

"There are two," Carina says. "Your extra key should be in here." She uses a small key to open a locked cabinet and slides out a tray with metal dividers. "It's not in here."

"My extra key is missing? So, anyone could have it?"

The panic in Landry's voice makes me instinctively want to put my arms around her to calm her, which would be a really stupid fucking thing to do right now. "Don't worry about it," I say. "I'll rekey the lock again."

"Thanks," she says with a relieved smile. "I'm glad we realized my extra key is missing now before I moved in. My original key could've fallen out of my skirt onto your floor, though. You might want to check. If it did, you could at least get in now, and do the rekey later."

I don't think my eyes could get any wider. Does she even realize what she said?

Carina's brows are arched to the rafters. Her eyes flit between me and Landry.

"Oh," I say. "You mean you think maybe it fell out when you borrowed my bathroom?"

I see the realization hit. Landry looks like she might pass out from the shock of her own slip up. "Right," she says. "Because of the problem with my toilet."

We're both talking way too fast.

Carina cocks her head and looks at Landry in confusion. "Don't you have two bathrooms in your unit?"

"They're both broken," Landry says, as if that's at all plausible.

"Well, not broken," I interject, hoping to steer this explanation in a direction that makes sense. "I'm upgrading them because hers didn't get changed out in the renovation."

"Really?" Carina asks. "That's weird. I thought the whole unit was remodeled."

"Well, the toilets are in there, but they never got hooked up."

"Oh." This seems to appease Carina's curiosity. "Stupid little stuff like that always happens during a reno."

"Always." I run my hand through my hair. "Contractors are ready to move on to the next job by the time it gets to the final touches and things get overlooked."

"Tell me about it," Carina agrees. "In unit 712, they forgot to install a door handle."

"Wasn't that done by maintenance?" I ask. "They didn't really hire an outside contractor to hang doors, did they?"

"It was the shower door. They only installed a handle on the inside."

"What a bunch of fucking clowns."

"Right?" Carina laughs.

Okay, good. We're out of the danger zone. All's well that ends well.

At least the plumbing contractor made legitimate mistakes that help make my excuse about Landry's toilets believable. I appreciate their incompetence, even though it'll likely cause me problems soon enough.

Landry still looks like she might faint.

"You look like you need to eat," I say, trying to reduce the tension all around.

"What I need is caffeine."

"After that coffee I gave you this morning?"

"Are you kidding?" she says. "I couldn't even drink that it was so strong. I poured it out. Your tumbler's in my car. I'll bring it in when I—"

The runaway train of reality hits us both at the same time.

Twice? Twice in one morning we've fucked up like this? It's a good thing last night was a one-time encounter. This woman makes my mouth fall open and spill words like she's tortured them out of me.

There's no use even trying to put a spin on it this time. I turn on my heels and walk out of the office. Maybe it's shitty of me to leave Landry trapped there with Carina staring at her like that, but the office is her responsibility. I fixed her slip of the tongue. With any luck, she can fix mine.

I'm going to rekey a lock and hang some fucking shelves in the meantime. Right after I unclog a drain.

Landry

How long can I stare at my feet? I suddenly realize it's so easy to explain. Carina's eyes are still on me when I look up and start talking.

"I brought over some boxes this morning, and Vaughn helped me bring them in. I mentioned I was going to run to Starbucks but he offered me coffee to save me the trip. Remind me to never take him up on that offer again." I laugh, but even I know it sounds scripted. "Anyway, long story short, I had to pour out the jet fuel he gave me, and go buy myself a drinkable latte instead."

"Yeah, he looks like he probably drinks strong coffee." She smiles as she puts the keys back in the locked cabinet.

"Oh, the strongest. You can't even imagine. It's so bad. I don't see how anyone—"

"Hey, Landry." She turns and shakes her head. "You don't really need to keep trying to explain why your key could possibly be on his floor or how he gave you a tumbler full of coffee before work. In fact, we could just ignore this morning's comments completely, you know? Like in court, when a judge says to strike something from the record."

"Right," I say. "Strike it from the record, Sally!" *What? Who the fuck is Sally? Why do I keep saying such stupid shit?* I stop pointing at the invisible court reporter and swallow hard. "I think that sounds like a really good plan."

"Great. But before we let it go completely, can I say one thing?"

"Sure."

"Whatever did or didn't happen between you and Vaughn, I'm pretty sure any other woman alive would've done exactly the same thing. Or not." She winks.

I knew I liked her the moment I met her. "Thanks, Carina."

"Actually, can I also ask a question, even though it's absolutely none of my business and totally inappropriate?"

"Mind-blowingly fantastic."

"Yeah, I figured." She smiles. "So, anyway, we have some leases coming up for renewal. I normally send out an email reminder, and we offer specials for longer renewals. Should we go over those?"

"Please."

We make it through all the renewals before lunch, and our afternoon is spent showing apartments. I'd normally let Carina handle the showings, but people just keep coming in. We'll never get to close if I don't take a few.

They almost all want a two-bedroom unit. We don't have any of those available right now, and our waitlist is approaching a laughable number. Everyone wants to see a unit to check out the new finishes, anyway. The owners are running a massive ad campaign about the renovations, which is silly because we're close to being fully occupied. I've never worked anywhere that was at one-hundred percent capacity. They really should cancel the ad at this point. It's worked almost too well.

Carina and I have our purses on our shoulders and are about to head out when our last visitor of the day arrives—not walking, slithering.

Lolita isn't wandering on her own today. Vonnie is right behind her, just watching the snake stroll into the office independently like a proud parent watching their toddler lead the way. It's all I can do not to jump up onto my desk, but I hold my ground. *She's not venomous. You can do this.*

Vonnie bends to pick up her forked-tongue companion. As the snake coils around her thin waist, she looks to me and says, "Well, I heard you met the resident son of a bitch this morning."

"Autry McDaniel? He was incredibly nice."

"He's a son of a bitch." She pulls out a chair and takes a seat. In front of my desk. I sit back down.

Carina locks the door to keep any other tenants or potential residents from coming in. Then she drops her purse on her own desk. "You want a glass of wine, Vonnie?"

"You know I can't turn down a nice glass of vino."

We don't have any nice vino, just cheap boxed wine. We offer new tenants a glass when they sign their lease. It's not champagne. It's not even sparkling. It's flat and too sweet and I'm definitely having a glass if I have to sit here and stare down a snake. I smile, remembering Autry asking, "which one?" this morning.

"Why don't you like Mr. McDaniel?" I ask.

"Honey, I'm old. I can't waste what precious life I have left talking about that insufferable little man."

She's the one who brought him up. I take one of the three wine glasses Carina has placed on my desk. When we each have one in our hand, Vonnie proposes a toast. "To soft kisses and hard dicks!"

Carina lifts her glass to clink with Vonnie's. They each take a drink. I chime in late, and try to pretend like she hasn't shocked me at all. She side-eyes me, while rubbing her snake's head on her cheek.

Is this woman fucking with me about Vaughn? Does she know? She can't know. I'm paranoid. I swear that damn snake is smiling at me. No, more like smirking.

Why did Vonnie and I get off to such a bad start? I'm nice. People like me, dammit. We need to start over, and I need to be the bigger person and make the first move.

"What's your best memory from your burlesque days, Vonnie?"

Staring at me like I've just asked the dumbest question she's ever heard, she replies, "The soft kisses and the hard dicks, honey." She cackles. Carina laughs along with her, so I join in, probably a beat too late. Again.

Trying to ingratiate myself, I add, "Hard kisses aren't always awful either."

Without acknowledging my comment, Vonnie turns the tables on me. "What's your best memory about this week so far?" She narrows her eyes at me. Now I'm sure she knows, but I have to play it cool.

"Well, I don't know if *best* is the word I'd use, but my most memorable moment would have to be meeting Lolita yesterday." I laugh, but I catch Carina's worried look in my peripheral vision. What? What did I say wrong?

"Oh, you'll get used to her," Vonnie says, standing and moving toward me. What's happening? No, no, no, no, no . . . "Here, you want to hold her?"

Breathe. Breathe. I can't do it. My body flies out of my chair like I've been ejected. My back is flat against the wall, and I'm genuinely struggling to breathe. Vonnie hands Lolita off to Carina, and comes to my aid with a fresh bottle of water. "Honey, take a sip. It's okay. What do you see?"

All I can see is her giant, beaded hoops, swinging to and fro. "I like your bold earrings," I manage to say.

"Thank you. I like your dainty, little, uptight studs, too. Take a drink for me, sweetie." She moves the bottle to my mouth, and I do as she's asked. "You should've told me you had an actual phobia. I just thought you were being a prissy little chicken shit."

I can't stop my laughter. She's so brutal. Who says things like that? No filter. No nuance. Just her raw thoughts, charging right out of her mouth. "Yeah," I say, wiping my eyes. "I think what I have is slightly more phobia than chicken shit."

"All right then. Well, me and Lolly are going to stay on this side of the desk, and you can get used to her in baby steps."

"Baby steps and distance sound like a much better idea."

I don't know if Carina opened a fresh box of wine or if my tastebuds have all been scared out of my mouth, but it's more palatable now. Lolita stays on her side of the desk, and I stay on mine.

Vonnie settles in and shares stories from her burlesque days, her face lighting up like a Christmas tree while she relives the moments. It's obvious she loved every minute of it. She misses it. Her name on the marquees, the lights, the audiences, the travel. The attention. The adoration. Never married, no kids—her greatest connections with people happened on the stage, and backstage, if all her stories are true. I'd bet on every one of them being at least partly true.

My mom always told me that even if I didn't like someone, if I could find one thing to admire about them, I could tolerate them. As I sit here, sipping cheap wine and listening to Vonnie recount her exploits, I think the things I initially didn't like about her are quickly becoming the very things I admire.

She might be the most authentic person I've ever met. Authentically offensive, sometimes, but that's still real. And oddly, charming.

Carina says she has to go, but part of me wants to stay, even though I definitely need to go. I still have packing to do. Vonnie stands and says, "Oh, I need to scoot, too. I've just been in here bending your ears and ignoring all my responsibilities."

That breaks my heart. She doesn't have any responsibilities. I vow on the spot that any time she shows up at closing and wants to tell her stories, I'll stay and listen. I'll drink cheap, shitty wine and let her regale me with her glory days for as long as she wants.

After Carina sprints off for the stairs to the garage, I linger be-hind and walk slowly down the hall with Vonnie. When we reach the door, she says, "Keep your wits about you, honey."

"What do you mean?"

"I see the way he looks at you. And who could blame him? And I see the way you look back at him when you think no one's looking."

"I've only been here two days."

"And one night."

Do not show a reaction to that. "Actually, I don't move in until this weekend."

"Oh, don't you *actually* me, you sweet summer child. I have been alive far too long. There's a difference between fucking some-one, and fucking *with* someone. Always be clear about which one you're doing, and which one's being done to you."

"That's good advice, but Vaughn and I aren't doing either one of those things with each other."

"Oh, okay, then. Well, you have a nice night." She turns around and heads for the elevators. I don't think she believes me, and I'm probably way more offended by that than I should be, given that I did just lie right to her face. But it's also none of her business.

Lolita looks back at me over Vonnie's shoulder, flicking her tongue. Smirking.

Vaughn

THESE SHELVES ARE TURNING out better than I expected, but there's nobody here to tell me how good they look. Holden went home hours ago. I'm tempted to send Landry a picture of the progress, but I want her to be surprised.

It was worth sacrificing some of the maintenance budget to buy the right materials. Plus, now there's plenty of the property's crappy shelves available for second bedroom office conversions. When all's said and done, this might actually look pretty damn close to what she imagined. Minus the ladder. I shake my head and laugh as I smear wood putty over a nail hole. *Her own fucking library.*

I'll have to ask her in the morning if she wants her shelves stained or painted. That's all that's left to do. I stand back and admire my work. Shit, this looks great. It's not like I have anything else to do tonight. I'm texting her now.

Me: *Do you want your bookshelves painted or stained?*

Landry: *I didn't know I'd get a choice. So exciting! Painted white, please. High gloss. But wait before you hang them. I want to paint the wall behind them first.*

She can't be serious. My thumb hits the screen, ready to unleash my pissed off reply, but I take a breath, remind myself she doesn't know I've done all this. She's expecting a few individual shelves hung on the wall. I snap a picture.

Me: *Too late. Hope you're not terribly disappointed.*

The little dots bounce like she's typing a reply. Then they stop. They bounce again. Stop again. She's killing me.

Landry: *Is that really in my apartment or are you fucking with me right now?*

Damn, how much of an asshole does she take me for? Yeah, never mind, I don't want to know the answer to that.

Me: *It's really in your apartment. I promise.*

Landry: *I can't believe you did that! I don't know what to say.*

Me: *Just give me the green light to start painting them.*

Landry: *Go for it!*

I imagine how big her smile is right now. If she were here, she'd probably spin around in front of these damn shelves. She looks at this whole apartment like it's a cathedral. It's a nice place, plenty of space and decent features, but her eyes widen like she's seeing arched beams and stained-glass saints.

Landry: *Should I come help?*

I really wish she wouldn't have asked that. Like it's not bad enough I'm already imagining her being here.

Me: *No, I've got it. Have a good night.*

Landry: *You think I'd just be in the way. I know how to paint.*

Me: *I have no doubt you can handle a paintbrush. But if you come back here, I highly doubt we'll get any painting done.*

Fuck! I shouldn't have sent that.

The dots are bouncing again.

Landry: *I hate to break it to you but those bookshelves are so sexy I probably wouldn't even notice you.*

Oh, she's good.

Me: *Ouch.*

I head back to my own apartment to make a sandwich and down a beer. I'm barely through the door when she texts again.

Landry: *Hey, Vaughn . . .*

Me: *Yeah?*

Landry: *Thank you.*

It defies logic that the smell of her could still be lingering in my place, yet, there it is. Sweet and spicy. Just like her. I should've stayed in her unit and ordered a damn pizza. Except pizza makes me think of her now, too. *Fuuuuck me.*

I don't even remember making this sandwich I'm halfway done eating, but I guess I'm the prime suspect on this half-empty beer, too. When I'm done with my dinner, I put a few bottles of water, and a few more beers, in a cooler with some ice. Pretty sure I'm going to be painting all night. If I keep a paintbrush in my hand, I can't text her again.

going to be painting all night. If I keep a paintbrush in my hand, I can't text her again.

Landry

I DON'T KNOW HOW long I've been sitting here on a box of books, staring at these gorgeous bare shelves and imagining them filled and decorated. But I'm not sure the paint is dry enough yet, and the last thing I want to do is mess them up. I'm scared to even touch them.

There are three more boxes of books still sitting on my backseat, but I got sweaty bringing up the first one, and I still have a full day of work ahead of me. I should probably go down to the office now.

The sound of my front door opening startles me for a few seconds, but then I realize it's either going to be Vaughn or Holden.

Vaughn's deep voice drifting down my hallway confirms it's him, and I can't help but smile. I stand and walk to the door of my unofficial library, lean against the frame, and watch him. He's singing along to whatever he's listening to through his earbuds. I don't recognize it.

"Holy fuck!" He yanks out an earbud and jumps when he sees me. "You scared the shit out of me! What are you doing in here?"

"I live here."

"Not yet, you don't!" His expression changes and he bursts into laughter. "You came in early to look at your bookshelves, didn't you?"

"I could hardly sleep! Of course, I had to come see them." I push off the doorframe, and take a sip from my coffee that's gone lukewarm in the paper cup. I've definitely been here longer than I thought. "They're perfect, Vaughn. Thank you so much. I didn't put anything on them yet because I wasn't sure if I could."

"No!" he bellows. "Do not put anything on them. The paint needs to harden. It'd be best if you gave them a full week, but I doubt you'll be able to go the whole weekend without shoving books on them."

"Those are the very first boxes I'm unpacking."

He looks at the box in the middle of the room. "Is that books?"

"Yeah. There are three more in my car. I should've packed them in smaller boxes."

"We have a hand truck. If you want to use it after work, just let me know."

"Thanks! Speaking of work, I should get to it." I step forward and hug him. "I really love them, Vaughn."

He hugs me back, and the last thing I want to do now is go to work. I shouldn't have wrapped my arms around him to begin with because I could stay right here all day. Why does this have to feel so good? So right.

"I'm glad you like them." His voice is low, and I can feel his heartbeat through his bright magenta shirt that looks good on him, no matter what he thinks.

I can't end this embrace, but one of us has to do it. Vaughn releases his hold on me. Thank goodness he has the clarity to do what's right.

But then comes the kiss.

The taste of his strong coffee is on his tongue, and his sculpted arms are around me again. I can't even blame him for initiating it because we leaned toward each other simultaneously. Like magnets.

We end the kiss together, the same way we started it. "This is going to be a problem, isn't it?" I ask through a weak laugh.

"Only if you want it to be."

"I do. I want it to be a problem right now." I plant a feather-light kiss on his lips, and I can feel the feral energy coming off him, but he doesn't kiss back. He's practically shaking under the effort to restrain himself, and I want to break him, make him lose control. "What happened? Don't you like me, anymore?" I tease.

"I like you entirely too much."

"Maybe you should fuck me like you hate me instead, so we can both get to work on time." I reach for his belt buckle. "You know, just this once?"

He pushes my hand away and unbuckles his own belt. His stiff cock is free before I'm done pulling up my skirt. "Turn around and put your hands on the wall." I do as he's said, and he immediately takes my panties to my ankles.

His open palm stings my ass, and I'm still reeling from the shock of it when he says, "Just so we're clear, if you really want to keep doing this, you should know this won't be the last time I fuck you hard and fast."

"Okay."

He moves closer until his mouth is right next to my ear. "And it won't be the last time I slap this sweet, sexy ass either."

I've had guys slap my ass during sex before, but it's always felt more playful than punishing; not that Vaughn is making me feel like I'm being disciplined right now, but he's not playing either. I turn my head until my eyes find his. "You can do whatever you want."

His groan reverberates between us. "Careful with your words."

"I want to do a lot of things with you, but being careful isn't one of them."

"Spread your pretty legs, and offer me that perfect pussy."

My arousal gushes at his requests. I turn to face the wall again, spread my legs, and tilt my hips for him. The cool air meets the heat of my exposed pussy, and I know before his fingers ever slide across it exactly how wet I am for him.

His hands grip my hips and close in toward each other. He moves them down until his thumbs reach my labia, and pulls them in opposition to open me. "So fucking wet. God, that's beautiful."

I could stand here and let him admire me all day, praise my body, say every filthy thing that crosses his mind until my legs shake and I'm close to collapsing, but we don't have that kind of time. If I don't say something, he's going to take it slow and prolong the teasing. This has to be a quickie, but he's not going to make it one unless I push him. "You do remember we're on a tight schedule here, right?"

"Are we?" He plunges a thumb into my pussy, and I suck in a sharp breath. I shamelessly rock back, encouraging him to keep going. His thumb circles inside me but the rest of him is still, silent for a few moments while he enjoys making me squirm under the increasing pressure he's applying. "I don't want to interfere with your schedule. Maybe I should just pull your panties back up and let you get on with your day."

"Please don't."

"What do you want?"

"You know what I want."

"Tell me again. Say please."

"I want you to fuck me. Rough. Please." I swallow hard. "Please just fuck me like you hate me."

"No can do, sweetheart." His thumb glides up and into my ass before I can take my next breath. "I don't fuck women I hate." He resumes the same circular motion he'd been reaming my pussy with before.

"Then fuck me like you need me. Please."

"There we go. That's better." He positions the swollen head of his cock at my opening, and I feel my walls flutter in anticipation of taking him. "But I'm not the only who needs this, am I?"

"No. I need it, too." Jesus, I'm panting already. How much longer is he going to do this?

"Need what?"

I want to pull his fucking hair out right now. But also, I'm so turned on I could scream. "Your dick. Inside me. I need to feel your thick, hard dick stretching my tight, wet pussy. Please, just fuck me. Make me sorry I ever asked for it."

He slams forward so hard it forces all the air from my lungs. "No, I might leave you sore, but I'll never leave you sorry."

Usually, I'd rebuke that level of cocksure arrogance, but I'm too busy clutching at the wall, grasping for purchase as he pulls his hips and thrusts again, his thumb fucking my ass in synchronicity. He's using me, just like I told him to, but that's not all he's doing. He's undoing things he knows nothing about . . . helping me fuck them away. I'm using him as much as I'm being used.

I truly need something to hold onto now. He clutches my hip with one hand when my muscles start to clench around him. His single-handed hold is enough to keep me steady while he assumes a more even rhythm. It's still hard and fast but his timing is consistent, and consistency is definitely key. "Oh, God, yes!"

It's a good thing I don't have neighbors right next door because hearing me shriek like I just did would destroy any chance we have of keeping this a secret. We've not only broken that non-fraternization policy; we've shredded it and set it on fire.

I'm definitely going to be sore.

And I'm damn sure not sorry.

He tucks himself back into his underwear and pulls up his pants while I'm still recovering against the wall.

I gasp when he literally sweeps me off my feet. "What are you doing?"

"Carrying you across the hall so you clean up before work. Unless you have towels and washcloths here. Paper towels even?"

"No, I don't have any of those things here yet."

My skirt is still rucked around my waist and my panties are dangling from one ankle and he doesn't seem to realize he can't carry me out of my apartment like this. "Vaughn, stop! What if someone sees us?"

"They won't." He steps through my door, pausing to extend his foot behind him to keep it from slamming, clears the width of the exterior hallway in two quick steps, and walks us safely into his apartment.

"I can't believe you just did that."

"We've probably both taken each other a little by surprise this morning."

"You know what I meant. Put me down."

"Relax, gorgeous. Your exhibitionism went entirely unappreciated." He carries me into his bathroom before he sets my feet back on the ground. "Except by me." He opens the shower door and turns on the water.

"What are you doing?"

"Taking my second shower of the day. Wanna join me?"

"No, I can't. I don't have any of my stuff to get ready again. Plus, there's not time. I'm probably already late." My phone is back in my apartment with my purse. It suddenly occurs to me that I'm still standing in front of him with my skirt up and my panties down.

"You worry too damn much." He lets the warm shower soak a wash cloth, wrings it out, and hands it to me. After I take the cloth, he kisses the top of my head. "All that work I did to relax you, and here you are, uptight all over again."

I push him away from me. "Get in the shower."

Not going to lie, I absolutely waste a few extra minutes watching the hot water run down his body in chaotic rivulets before I force myself to clean up, adjust my clothes, and go back to my own apartment.

Stunned. Sore. Still not sorry.

The time on my phone confirms my fear. Fashionably late on day three.

"Where are the donuts?" Carina asks when I step into the office.

"What?"

"When you show up late, you're supposed to bring donuts."

"You have no idea what I would give for a donut right now." I hold up my nearly full cup of cold coffee. "And some hot coffee. I brought some boxes over, and lost track of time in my apartment. I forgot to even drink it."

"I made coffee. And I was just teasing. We have donuts."

"You are an angel. Best leasing agent ever." I dump my old coffee in the sink at the back of the office, and refill my cup from the fresh pot. The smell rises on the steam and I inhale.

Carina holds up a box of powdered donuts. "They're not hot. They're not fresh. But they're free."

"I haven't had one of those since I was a kid."

"They're the Autry McDaniel special. He drops off a box every few weeks. If he comes in and announces he has a little treat for us, you can always expect these donuts."

"That's really sweet."

"He's a total sweetheart. But don't tell Vonnie I said that. And if she comes in here, hide your donut. She will go on and on about what a cheapskate he is for giving us store-bought donuts when Shipley's is right down the street."

"Got it." I take a donut from the box and sit down at my desk. "Does Vonnie ever deliver any treats I should be aware of?"

"At Christmas, she gives out bottles of purple gin. It's pretty, but I hate gin, so I can't be a fair judge of the quality."

"I am a big fan of that purple gin. I guess I better try to get on her good side between now and Christmas." We laugh, sip our coffee, and nibble on our dry donuts while we both avoid our voicemails and emails for a few more minutes. There's a question that's been bugging me since I met her.

"Why didn't you move into my job when the old manager left?"

"I didn't want the job."

"What about assistant manager?"

"We've never had an assistant here. We're not big enough to need one. There were two leasing agents for a while, but I don't mind being the only one." She gets up to pour herself some more coffee. "Besides, I can't take a pay cut, and if I wasn't a leasing agent anymore, I'd lose my residuals and commissions."

"The owners can structure your pay however they want. It doesn't matter what your title is."

"I guess, but I'm happy like it is. It's not a big deal to me."

"What if I asked them to add assistant manager to your title so you're officially both? You do everything an assistant would do, so it's only fair that you get the title to go along with the responsibilities. It's good to have that on your resume, Carina. That way, if something were to happen here, you'd be able to apply for either job somewhere else."

Her face looks ashen. "Are you trying to tell me something, Landry? Am I not going to be here for much longer?"

"What? No, that's not what I meant at all. I hope you're going to be here. I need you here. Please don't quit."

"I don't plan on it. But I'm not getting fired, right?"

"No, definitely not."

"Okay. Cool."

The second bite of my donut is still whole in my mouth when a man I've never seen before walks into the office carrying what appears to be a ponytail of human hair. There is no head or further evidence of a human attached to it, just a pink hair tie binding a thick, wavy mass of dark hair. "I found this on the sidewalk," he announces.

"Damn," I say. "I hope that's not a serial killer's trophy that he accidentally dropped in his haste to flee the crime scene." I laugh. Alone. I laugh alone. And that should probably be the title of my memoir. "You can leave it here in case anyone comes looking for it."

Carina rescues me. "I'll put a message in the community forum. I bet someone got it cut off so they could donate it. They're going to be devastated when they realize it's missing, if they haven't already. Thank you so much for bringing it in."

The voluntary donation scenario actually makes sense. And no one is ever going to look at Carina like they're afraid of her now because she's said it out loud. Unlike me, over here spewing random thoughts about a potential serial killer on the premises. My first thought was to make a serial killer joke.

My second thought is how I can't wait to tell Vaughn about it. Somehow, I just know he won't be scared off by a serial killer joke. He'll laugh with me. Dark humor and rash decisions are kind of my brand, and I don't think either is entirely off-brand for Vaughn.

The guy hands the ponytail to Carina, and keeps his eyes turned away from me as he leaves. "Does he live here?" I ask as soon as he's gone.

Carina shrugs. "I've never seen him before. I hope he's not the killer."

Powdered sugar sprays from my mouth as I laugh.

This place may be exactly where I belong.

Vaughn

THE TENANTS HERE COMPLAIN about a lot of ridiculous shit, but they're apparently not wrong about the garage door being broken more often than it works. It's a high-speed door, and I don't mess with those, so now, my schedule's been hijacked by having to meet with a new vendor. Middle-of-the-day meetings piss me off.

At least the technician texted to let me know when he arrived like I asked. I got a list of all the property's approved vendors from Carina last week. Lucky for this guy, I don't have a preferred roll-up door guy. Most of the others on that list are getting replaced by my contacts. I'm loyal to people I know I can trust to get the job done.

Firm handshake. Okay, he's off to a good start. We make our official introductions, and he hands me his card. "You're new here," he says, as if I might not be aware.

"Yeah. Started last week. I hear this thing breaks down a lot. Is there anything we can do to change that?"

"I can get you a bid for a new system. This one's old. Needs to be replaced."

"Why?"

"I just told you. It's old."

"Can you still get parts for it?"

"Yeah, but that might not last much longer."

"Okay, but what's wrong with it today? And how can I be sure that same problem won't happen if we upgrade?"

"New equipment is always a better choice. Plus, it'll be under warranty so it'll save you money in the long run."

"I'm going to ask one more time. What specifically is better about the newer version? What changed?"

"Old equipment just breaks, man. That's life."

"How long have you been doing this job?" He can't be any older than Landry. Hell, he might be a few years younger.

"Long enough."

Wrong answer. "Thanks for your time."

"So, you don't want me to fix it?"

"You either don't understand this equipment or you think I'm too stupid to understand it. Either way, I asked you twice what the current problem was, and you couldn't give me an answer."

"I haven't even looked at it yet."

"But you know the whole system needs to be replaced?"

"Yeah, because it's old."

"I tell you what, when you're in charge of the budget, you buy all the new equipment you want. When I'm responsible for the spending choices, I prefer to make an informed decision." I hand his card back to him. "Do yourself a favor and find a new job. You're not cut out for this one."

He mutters "fuck you" under his breath as he's getting back into his truck, and it just makes me laugh. He's wasted enough of my time for one day.

I catch up with Holden and help him finish a make-ready on the second floor. The tenant who complained about the tacky hallway carpet must live on this floor. Casinos use calmer colors and more subdued patterns.

These units are all the smallest floorplans. Maybe they thought the wild carpet would appeal to younger tenants.

As we're locking up the apartment to leave, I ask how the screenplay is coming along.

"Good. I'm workshopping it this weekend."

I have no idea what that means, but he seems excited about it. "Cool. Hope that goes well for you."

"Yeah, me, too. Do you think it would be okay if I filmed something in this hallway? This carpet's dope."

"Maybe if you're *on* dope. And no, you cannot film anything anywhere on the property." I point to a security camera. "That's the only filming that can take place here."

"I always forget about those." He waves at the camera, like an idiot.

"Quit that."

I apparently forget about the security cameras sometimes, too. Like when I carried Landry bare-assed across the hallway between our apartments this morning. *Fuuuuck me.*

When that occurs to her—and somehow, I know it will—she is going to lose her shit. So, I've got that to look forward to.

My back was to the camera, though. The footage probably doesn't show anything. Except me carrying her across the hall from her apartment to mine. It's not like anyone is ever going to see it, anyway. And even if they did, we could just say she cut her foot and needed a bandage.

Yeah, sure, that would totally explain why her panties are dangling from her ankle.

"Hey, you know that lady with the snake has the hots for you, right?" Holden laughs.

"She's just flirty by nature." I shake my head. "Plus, I think she's lonely."

"Yeah, but are you going to go for it?"

"What the actual fuck is wrong with you?"

"Don't knock it, man. Older women can teach you things."

"Stop talking."

"Hey, I'm just saying it could work out for you. I'm thinking about trying my luck with the manager."

"Landry?"

"Yeah. How old do you think she is, like thirty?"

"She's twenty-five. And she's not going to give you the time of day. You know she could fire you, right?"

"Oh. She dresses so sophisticated. I figured she was older than that. But I thought you said only you can fire me."

"Are you trying to find out?"

"No." He stares at the carpet the rest of the walk to the elevator.

When the doors open, I stay put. "Go ahead. I'll catch the next one."

"Why?"

"For your safety."

Holden hops into the elevator. I wait for the doors to close before I let my head fall back. Staring at the ceiling, I actually feel bad for treating the kid like that. I've only known Landry for *three days*. Three days and I'm acting like she belongs to me. Nothing is ever going to happen between her and Holden. There was no reason for me to let his crush on her bother me. I need to get my head straight.

And that's going to require staying away from her for a while. What could be so hard about it? We just work together. Live right across the hall from each other. Have a physically magnetic attraction. Share the same sense of humor.

Her voice whispers in my ear as clearly as if she's just appeared out of thin air: *Then fuck me like you need me.*

Yeah, I'm going to have to move.

To another state.

At least.

It's a clear night. If there weren't so many lights from the streets and buildings, I'd be able to see all the stars. I pull a beer from the cooler, lean back in my chair, and stare out over the edge of the roof.

The only time I've ever seen a true-dark night sky was in a place I never want to see again. Desolate and devastated by day, but all those stars, though. I jump when the door opens. And then I relax because there's only one person it could be. I can tell myself I don't want to see her, but knowing she just walked through that door is the only thing that could've put this smile on my face.

"Hey, boss."

"Holden? What are you doing up here?" I turn and spot the camera equipment he's carrying, and the other two guys. "You have got to be kidding me."

"I didn't film anything inside, I swear. We just need a panoramic of the skyline. And a few shots of traffic and street signs from above. It's for a montage scene. Won't take five minutes."

"How'd you get up here?"

"You gave me this card, remember? When I had to bring the air-conditioning guys up here."

"I didn't intend for you to keep it." *Shit. I totally forgot I ever gave him that.*

"Oh, sorry. Tonight's the only time I've used it. I don't regularly come up here or anything."

He's lucky I do regularly come up here, so I know he's telling the truth. The other two guys are antsy, a couple of kids afraid they're about to get in trouble. "Go ahead. Get what you need, and leave that access card with me on your way out."

"Thanks, bro." I watch him and his friends set up, and listen to them talk about the shots. This place is just a paycheck until he can get somewhere else. He's got a passion. I never bothered to pick up one of those. If he calls me bro again, his might be short-lived.

It takes a lot longer than the promised five minutes, but they're packing up their gear, and I'm not about to forget to collect that access card this time. "Y'all want a beer?"

Aw, hell. They all look like they're afraid it was a trick question. "I'll trade you for that keycard."

Holden laughs, which is the cue the others need. He hands me the card and I open the cooler. They all grab one. I only have one chair set up so I stand, and we walk to the rail. "You take that footage for the workshop this weekend?"

"No, that's just for my script. What we shot tonight was for a short we're working on."

"Oh." I think I know what he means, probably like for YouTube or something. "Are y'all screenwriters, too?"

One of the guys nods his head. "Yeah, but I'm mainly focused on my YouTube channel right now."

There it is. "What do you do on it?"

"Debunk conspiracies, mostly."

"Okay. What about you?" I lean forward and look at the third guy.

"Yeah, I write in the same genre as Holden."

I've never asked Holden much about his writing. "What genre is that?"

"Horror," Holden says.

"That's what you're hoping to get ideas for while you're working here?"

"Ideas are everywhere."

"I'd rather my workplace not inspire any horror flicks."

"You can't stop inspiration," YouTube guy says. "Once it sparks, you've just got to go with it. If you ignore it, the muse might stop bringing it."

"The muse, huh? Maybe you could tell her you'd like some inspiration for a comedy instead."

"Nah," Holden says. "I'm not funny enough to write comedy."

"But you think you're scary enough to write horror?"

"You don't have to be scary to write it. You just have to be willing to live with fuck-up shit playing out in your head."

Nobody says anything to that. We just watch the city move and finish our beers.

Landry

Vaughn's been scarce since our unscheduled Wednesday morning meeting in my apartment. I'm sure he's busy. It's not like he has to check in with me or anything. I haven't brought over any more boxes, so I haven't even been up to our floor. I never put paint in my apartment with sticky notes like he said I could. I'm not avoiding him; it's just that I've been busy.

I haven't slept much the past few nights, but I'm sure it's just pre-move anxiety. So many little things have come up that I didn't plan for: running out of boxes (twice), deciding to donate so much more stuff than I'd originally intended, spending hours searching for a pool key I didn't know I'd lost, ignoring dozens of phone calls from my mom, and then having to reply to all her follow-up texts to explain why I didn't answer and reassure her that yes, my new apartment is safe.

Safe from what? Who knows what nightmare scenarios she imagines. I don't ask because I don't need her anxiety competing with mine for headspace.

Just after midnight last night, I tangled packing tape in my hair. I eventually gave up and went to bed—after I used a dull pair of scissors to saw off a small section at the nape of my neck. I was exhausted and in no shape to keep battling the twisted mass of tape and hair, and tears were verging, so I just hacked away at the problem. Let's just say I won't be wearing my hair up anytime soon.

Tonight, I plan to approach the tape gun with caution, seal up my last few boxes, create dinner from whatever odds and ends need to be eaten out of my fridge and pantry, and faceplant into my bed by nine p.m.

Carina takes the coffee pot out of my hand as I'm about to pour myself another cup. "More caffeine isn't the answer," she says. "You need to touch grass."

"What?"

"You're yawning and irritable. Go walk in the fresh air and sunshine. Slip your shoes off, and step into the grass, feel the earth beneath your feet, and get grounded."

"If you start inviting me to meditation classes, I will be forced to fire you."

"Mediation works."

"I knew it. You're one of them."

"Guilty. Now, go outside. Listen to the birds, look at the flowers. It'll help, I promise."

The Nouveau does have nice landscaping and some open green spaces with lush grass. Maybe she's right. I retake control of the coffee pot, and pour a cup for my walk. "Fine. I'll go try your new age wisdom, but I'm taking coffee."

"Watch out for snakes." Her laughter is evil, but playful at the same time, and it makes me laugh, too.

"If I see a snake, it's getting doused in hot coffee."

"Well, that sounds like a great way to piss one off." She laughs again. "I thought you grew up in the country."

"Longing to live in the city. Where I thought there wouldn't be snakes."

I push my way out the door, listening to her laughter fade as a warm breeze hits my face. The sun is so bright I have to squint, but the smell of honeysuckle is intoxicating. There are vines growing on the iron fence that lines the sidewalk, and a group of kids walking home from the private middle school down the street stops to pick some. I watch as they carefully pull out the thread and suck the nectar, just like I did a million times when I was their age. Add that to the list of things I didn't expect to find in the city.

One of the girls puts her hands up to her nose and inhales. She smiles like it's her favorite smell in the world. It's a good one. They pick a few more and move on, reabsorbed in their conversations and jokes.

I make my way over to the fence, slip off my shoes, and stand in the grass, letting a few bees enjoy the vines before I reach for a blossom. It's such delicate work to taste that one tiny drop of nectar, but so worth it.

Whether it's the grass beneath my feet or the honeysuckle in the air and on my tongue, I don't know, but I do feel better.

When I look up, a couple older girls are coming down the sidewalk. They look like highschoolers, and I'm pretty sure they should probably still be on campus for another hour, but I'm not their parents or the cops, so what do I care?

As they pass, I notice the brunette's short hair is rough and uneven in the back—like someone chopped off her ponytail. A fleeting image of the hair in Carina's desk tells me it's a perfect match.

"Hey!" I yell. "Did you just get your hair all cut off?"

The girls stop and turn around. "Yeah," the brunette says. "Why?"

"I think we might have your ponytail in the office."

"Okaaaay." The girls exchange glances.

"Do you want it back?"

"Why would I want it back?"

"I thought maybe you cut it off to donate it."

"No. I cut it off because I was tired of it."

"And then you just left it on the ground?"

"Yeah." She shrugs.

"Well, someone found it and brought it inside."

She shrugs again, more dramatically this time. "Freaks are everywhere."

"That's a lot of hair. It could probably be used to make wigs for people who've lost their own hair."

"Great. Give it to those people. I never want to see it again." She shakes her head from side to side. "It's gone and there's nothing anybody can do about it."

Her friend's face lights up. "Aw, man. You should've framed it and given it to your dad as a going away present."

"Fuck him. I'm not giving him anything. He can look at the back of my head and accept that his rules no longer apply to me. That can be his present."

Oh, my God. This angry little rebel is out here walking around looking like a pack of rats gnawed off her ponytail just to piss off her dad. Her spiteful energy makes my soul sing.

I would've never had the guts to do what she's done, but I absolutely understand the satisfaction she's feeling as she swishes the ragged tips of her hair across the nape of her neck. She's free, at least of that one oppressive thing.

The breeze kicks up again, and it catches my long strands and swirls them at the side of my face. I was raised in a house where girls were expected to have long hair, too. Right now, I like it being long, but when I was her age, I would've given anything for the freedom to experiment with it.

"Okay," I say. "Well, if you're sure you don't want it, I'll see if I can donate it somewhere."

"Go for it." She spreads her arms wide and spins down the sidewalk, the same way I spun around in my new apartment. "I'm freeeeee!" Her friend runs to catch up to her. Giggles erupt from the tough exteriors they're trying so hard to project.

I watch them go as I step back into my shoes and wonder how long she'll leave the edges jagged like that. Deep in my core, I envy her grit, but I worry for the hurt that fosters it, too.

Damn. When did I get old enough to worry about teenagers?

Carina is ending a phone call when I come back inside. "Feel better?"

"So much better." I dump the rest of my coffee into the sink and switch to water. "I met the girl who used to be attached to that ponytail in your desk."

She opens the drawer. "Oh, yay! I bet she's so glad we have it."

"She doesn't give a damn who has it. But she's cool with us donating it."

"My cousin's a hair stylist. I know she does donation cuts sometimes."

"Perfect. Those karma points are all yours."

"Listen to you, talking about karma. You'll be my yoga buddy in no time."

"I cardio and I weight train. I don't yoga."

"Yoga can be cardio, trust me. And you weight train with your own resistance." She flexes her bicep.

"I'm never going to be a yogi."

The last few hours of the day drag because all I can think about is getting home. We finally make it to closing time with no upset tenants, no snakes, and still no sign of Vaughn.

Carina tucks the ponytail into an envelope. "Don't want to walk out holding this like I just took it off someone's head."

"Or get pulled over and have the cops see it on your passenger seat."

"Don't curse me like that! Good luck with the move." She slides the envelope into her purse. "Remember, you can no longer use traffic as an excuse for being late to work."

"Please, give me some credit. I'm way more creative than that."

I've spent the whole day eager to get out of here and finish packing, but now all I want to do is go upstairs. I linger in the office for a while after Carina's gone.

It occurs to me I probably should go up to my apartment and put sticky notes on the floor to show the movers where the furniture goes. They did that on one of those real estate reality TV shows one time. But I think that was a move where the owners weren't going to be there when the movers arrived. I'll be here.

Maybe I should go up and check all the appliances. I haven't done that yet. It's after closing time on Friday. Vaughn isn't going to fix anything for me over the weekend, so what's the point?

Then again, he probably would if I asked. But I don't think I need anything fixed. What if I do, though?

The elevator doors open before I even press the button. It's a sign. Clearly, I'm supposed to go up there.

<h1 style="text-align:center">Vaughn</h1>

THE ONE DAY I knock off a little early to work out and I run into Landry in the hallway. I'm coming out of my apartment and she's wiggling the key into her lock. A few more minutes and we'd have completely missed each other.

My hair's wet from my shower, and I'm wearing shorts. It's fairly obvious I didn't just get home. Her eyes lock on mine for a moment. "Got a date?"

"Yeah. With the grocery store."

"You know you can get groceries delivered, right?"

"And pay a delivery fee plus a tip? You know that's a waste of money, right?"

"Worth every penny. Don't give me any shit when you see mine being delivered."

"No promises." After tomorrow, she'll live here. Right across the hall. I'll see her groceries being delivered, know when she comes and goes . . . who comes and goes with her. "You need any help moving tomorrow? Sorry, I probably should've offered before."

"No. I've got movers scheduled. But thanks."

"Sure." If it's going to be this awkward every time we run into each other in the hallway, living here after she moves in is going to be a lot less convenient. "Well, let me know if you need anything. I'll be around most of the day tomorrow."

"Okay. Have fun going to the grocery store in rush-hour traffic."

"It's only a few blocks away."

"Yeah, but if you wait a few hours, it'll take half the time to get there."

If I wait a few hours, I'll need another shower, because all I want to do is follow her into her apartment and pick up where we left off last time I was in there. "Be safe driving home tonight."

"I will."

Whoa, that sounded snappy. Why'd her whole demeanor just change? Was she asking me to come inside, and now she thinks I rejected her? Shit. I was too busy remembering her naked with her hands on the wall, her hair cascading down her back, her ass—

"Hey, you never provided that paint like we talked about." I run my hand through my hair to push it off my forehead. "But if you want any help painting after you move in, I could maybe be persuaded."

"Maybe, huh? Enjoy the grocery store, Vaughn." She pushes her door open, goes inside, and lets it slam behind her.

The fuck was that? I offer to help her do something and she slams the door in my face?

Landry's car is already gone from her spot in the parking garage when I get back from the store. I guess I'll give her the flowers tomorrow. Maybe she'll be in a better mood by then. They're just a housewarming gift. Just welcome to the building flowers. Just maybe don't slam the door in my face anymore flowers. *Fuuuuck me.*

Landry

I can't believe I woke up before dawn for a move that took less than three hours in total. The movers showed up at my old place at eight. It's not even noon yet, and I'm completely moved in. There are boxes in every room that I still need to unpack, but all my stuff is here now. This is officially home.

From my couch, all I can see through my windows are other buildings and clouds. I'm too high up to even see treetops. It's strange and wonderful, and still a little unbelievable. I mentally scroll through the tasks ahead. Sheets, blanket, and pillows need to be put on the bed. I'm not tired at the moment, but I know when the exhaustion hits, the last thing I'm going to want to do is make the bed. The bathroom needs to be unpacked, at least enough so I have what I need to shower. Groceries have to be ordered.

I make the bed and put the necessities in the shower while groceries are on the way. I know once I open the boxes of books and start filling my shelves, that's where I'll spend the rest of my day, so I'm trying to avoid the library altogether until I have all the basic necessities situated. But after the groceries are put away, it's going to be me, charcuterie, and a bottle of wine, unpacking books and filling bookshelves until I'm too tired to lift my arms. Bliss.

Slicing cheese means unpacking the knives, and if I'm going to unpack those, I may as well decide which drawer the silverware should go in and put it all away. And I need a wine glass, so why not unpack all the glasses and put those away, too?

I snack on grapes as I slide glasses into place in the cabinet. All I need now is a cutting board and a plate, which, of course, leads to more unpacking.

When I've finally found everything that I need, I fan several loosely ruffled pieces of prosciutto around the edge of my plate, add two sections of cheese cubes, and fill in the center with grapes. I forgot to leave room for crackers. Why is there never room for crackers? Great, now I need a bowl.

It's a balancing act, but I manage to carry my lunch into the library in one trip. I set it all on the antique desk that was my grandmother's, pour myself a glass of wine, and raise a toast to her. Along with the desk, she left me a collection of vintage romance novels. It seems only fitting to unpack those first. I position her framed photo on the same shelf. She really loved those books. And me. "Cheers, Gran!"

I need a ladder to fill the upper sections, and since my custom shelves didn't come with one, I guess I have to go across the hall and ask if a certain maintenance man has one that I can use. The tenants here probably ask for things like that all the time. I'm sure it's not a big deal.

Vaughn is shirtless when he opens his door. Does he ever wear a shirt when he's home? "Do you have a ladder I can borrow?"

"Yes, I have a ladder. No, you cannot borrow it."

"Why not?"

"Because day drinking and ladder climbing don't mix."

"What makes you think I've been drinking?"

"Your lips are wine-stained."

Stop looking at my mouth.

His thumb traces my bottom lip and pulls gently. "You chew on your lip when you're stressed, don't you?"

When I snap myself out of the shocked paralysis of him thumbing my mouth, I slap his hand away. "I don't know. Why?"

"Because that's where the wine has turned it red, the raw and swollen places."

Is he trying to be dirty? Because that sounded dirty. It *felt* dirty.

"I've had half a glass. I'm putting my books on the shelves and I can't reach the top ones because *someone* wouldn't give me a ladder on a rail, which would've been a totally safe option at any time."

"I'll bring a ladder over and you can hand the books up to me."

I don't want him to arrange my books; I want to do it myself. "Is it your birthday?"

"My birthday?"

I point to the bar-height section of kitchen countertop where the vase is sitting. "Someone sent you flowers. What's the occasion?"

"Oh. Those are for you, actually."

"For me?" I stand stupefied in his doorway, watching his back muscles as he walks away.

He's just as mesmerizing on the return. "Here. Welcome to the building. Officially."

"Wow. Thanks. They're beautiful."

"You're welcome. Let me put on a shirt, and I'll go to the supply room and grab a ladder."

"Okay. I'll just go put these in water." *They're already in water, you idiot. They're in a vase full of water.* "I mean, I'll put them in my apartment. Anyway, that's where I'll be. In my apartment. You don't have to knock. The door will be unlocked. Just come on in. Don't forget the ladder." *Oh, my God! Stop talking!* I wince. He probably wonders who ties my shoes for me at this point. "So, I'll see you in a few."

I walk backwards the entire way across the hall to my own door. In my defense, Vaughn's naked chest and torso are really freaking hard to look away from.

Once I'm safely back in my own place, I set the vase on my counter and stare at it like no one has ever given me flowers before.

Because they haven't.

I had a whole husband and never once got flowers, not even when a stereotypical asshole like him might've been expected to give me some. I'm glad he didn't. This is one perfect thing that no tainted memories of him or anyone else can fuck up. My first flowers aren't apology flowers. They're beautiful.

Vaughn walks right through my door without knocking—exactly like I told him to do, but it startles me. And he's just caught me standing in the middle of the room, smiling at a vase of flowers like I'm under the influence of something a lot stronger than half a glass of wine. He has to think I'm a lunatic at this point.

"Hey!" I practically shout the word, before nodding at the ladder he's carrying. "Oh, good. You found one."

"Yeah, I found this lost ladder in the supply room, right where I'd put it." He laughs. "Where would you like me to put it now?"

"What?"

He hoists the ladder a few feet for reference.

Oh, right. The ladder. "Follow me." *Follow me? Really?*

Without waiting for any more of my brilliant instructions, he sets the ladder against the shelves. It's the perfect height. I wonder if he has other ladders of varying sizes. He probably does. A ladder for every occasion.

I pass him a stack of three books using two hands. He takes them all in one of his. And then he roughly shoves them onto the shelf.

"Easy. You'll dent the corners."

His smile is sexy, even when he's so close to laughing at me. "Sorry. I'll be gentler from now on."

"Thank you." I hand him three more. He one-hands them again, but he's more careful pushing them into place.

We repeat this process a few more times, and then I lift a stack and say, "Lay these flat."

"Not upright?"

"No, I want them to lay stacked on the shelf just like this."

"Why?"

"Because I like the way shelves look when there are random stacks here and there. And look how pretty these spines are. I want them showcased."

"Okay." He takes them from me and uses two hands to align their edges so they're perfectly neat after he's set them down. So attentive. "Like that?"

"Yeah, that looks good." I hand up a white ceramic elephant with its trunk and one front foot raised. "Set this on top of them."

"Why a stampeding elephant?"

"He's not stampeding. He's trumpeting. They do that when they're happy."

Vaughn turns the elephant from side to side in his hand, scrutinizing it like he's an expert in elephant behavior. "If you say so."

"Move him a few inches to the right."

There is an audible grunt, but he does what I've asked.

His arm extends with his hand open, ready for me to fill it with another stack of books.

"Turn him an inch or so to the left," I say, still staring at the elephant.

Vaughn sighs, reaches up again, and pushes the whole elephant to the left.

"No, put him back where he was, but turn him a few inches so his trunk is more visible from down here."

"I'm not down there. I'm up here. So I have no fucking idea how visible his trunk is to you."

"Which is why I'm giving you such detailed guidance."

"That elephant is exactly where he wants to be. Look how happy he is. He's trumpeting. More books, please."

I give him another stack, and we continue until that shelf is filled. He climbs down and moves the ladder over a few feet to start on the next section. My eyes keep going back to the elephant, but I don't say anything. Maybe I'll learn to like him in that position. We'll see.

Vaughn groans when he reaches for books and his hand meets glass instead.

"You're going to need two hands for this."

He looks down and shakes his head at me. "What the hell is that?"

"It's a glass peony. Isn't it gorgeous? It matches the two smaller ones on that shelf." I nod toward a lower shelf that he can't possibly see unless he morphs into a human pretzel.

"Why can't it go down there on the same shelf as the others?"

"Because it's perfect for that top corner." I shove the large pink glass flower at his hand again, but he doesn't take it this time either. "I don't like things to be too matchy-matchy. All three peonies on one shelf would be too much."

He reluctantly takes the flower and sets it into place. "How are you even going to get up here to dust all this stuff?"

"I guess I'll have to call someone who has a ladder to come do it for me." I wink up at him when he glances down to side-eye me.

"I'll give you a key to the supply room. You can borrow the ladder anytime."

"I couldn't borrow it today."

"Today, you got me and the ladder."

"Um, can you turn it a few inches that way?"

"Which way, Landry? I don't have eyes in the back of my head."

You could turn your damn head and look at me again to see what I meant. "To the right."

The ladder rattles a bit as he starts down it, thinking he's done.

"No, Vaughn. My right, not yours."

"We're facing the same goddamn direction! Your right is my right!" He sighs again, but his feet travel back up the rungs. "Like this?"

"Almost. Pull it forward an inch."

"What the hell difference will an inch make?"

"Do you really need me to explain that?"

Oh, sure. Now you can turn around and look at me.

I've never seen anyone who wasn't falling descend from a ladder so quickly.

His feet hit the floor, his body turns, and his hands grab my hips and pull me against him all in one swift move. But when his mouth goes to my neck and begins to make its way up toward my ear, he takes his time, letting me discern every touch of his lips, his tongue, his teeth . . . each move far less than an inch.

A chill spreads across my shoulders and down my arms, causing his breath to feel hotter against my skin. My nipples pebble at the increased sensation, and a sudden rush of arousal soaks my panties. I crave his touch in more places than two hands and one mouth could possibly cover, but I'm absolutely down for him to try.

He lifts my feet off the ground, and I wrap my legs around his waist, rocking my wetness against his hard cock as my head falls aside to give him better access to my neck. "Please don't stop doing that."

"Not even to wreck your sheets?" He asks, barely separating his mouth from my skin.

"What you're doing right now could probably wreck my sheets."

His laughter reverberates between his lips and my neck. "What are we doing in the library when there are sheets to wreck?" He carries me down the hall to my room, still scraping his teeth across my skin as we approach the doorway, bump into it, and bounce off. He stops at my bed. "Kneel on the mattress for me."

My arms fall from his neck, and I unwrap my legs from his hips. With his hands on my ribcage, he steadies me until my shins meet the comforter. I rest my weight there, kneeling in front of him and already missing his warmth.

He pulls his shirt over his head and then removes mine. His fingers toy with the straps of my bra, dancing them down my arms, tickling and teasing. My pussy clenches, and my breath catches as he reaches around my back to undo the clasp. He uses both hands, and as soon as the tension releases, he pulls the satin and lace from my body as if he's unwrapping a present, his eyes anxiously anticipating the reveal.

He's seen me before, but he makes me feel like seeing me now is new all over again. His thumbs rub across my nipples and the contact has me bordering on euphoria. How does he send me into such a heightened state so fast? We're both still fully clothed from the waist down, and if he doesn't make moves to correct that soon, I will.

As if he can read my mind (or my body), he says, "Lie back and scoot down until your ass is at the edge of the mattress." He drops to his knees at the side of the bed, and mine turn to jelly. I follow his instructions.

I watch my panties slide down my legs, looking like nothing more than a scrap of lace in his big hands. Those strong hands push my weak knees apart and hold them spread wide for him, my bent legs supported only by his grasp as he lifts them from the mattress. "Put your feet on my shoulders and relax."

The moment I do, he leans forward and gives my pussy the same attention he'd shown my neck before we hit the doorframe. My back arches.

His hands glide up and down my thighs, warming me. I relax as much as I possibly can with his mouth working me over like this, like he could devour me. Like he hasn't already in too many ways.

My sheets are spared because his face takes the brunt of my release. He lifts my feet from his shoulders and sets them on the edge of the bed. When he rises up and shoves his shorts down his hips and thighs until they fall to the floor, I can't stop looking at his glistening beard, the way his eyes are hooded now, and his brow is heavier. I don't know if I've ever known a man who's face literally radiates lust the way his does.

He's raw in ways I haven't experienced before. I'm by no means innocent, but there's a primal edge to his sexuality. Not frightening. Thrilling.

"Are you going to slide back and make room for me on the bed? Or are you asking me to take you like this?" He gathers both my ankles in one hand and pulls my legs straight up in the air.

"You could always start like this, and we could just see where it goes."

"I know where it goes." He separates my ankles, one in each hand now, and holds my legs in a wide V as he presses the swollen crown of his cock against my opening. His hips rock forward, guiding the tip upward through my arousal before he brings it back down and begins to push inside my orgasm-tightened pussy. "Damn, are you going to let me in?" he teases.

"What's the password?" I tease back.

"Did my tongue misspell it? It sure seemed like I was spelling it right."

I laugh at his arrogance—and the accuracy. And then I fist the comforter because I know by his fading smile that he's done teasing. His hips press forward, forcing his full erection inside me.

"God, yes, that hurts so good." I can't move to match his rhythm yet. My body needs a minute to adjust to the way he's stretching me, his hard cock filling me so completely.

"I love that you like it a little rough sometimes."

"Only because I trust you."

"You should never share your body with a man you don't trust."

"I don't." *Not anymore.*

I rock my hips up to meet his next thrust, and I catch a glimpse of his smile before his head falls back and his enraptured groan fills the room.

Just when I think he's close, he stops thrusting and tells me to move up on the mattress. He follows. Once we're positioned with both our bodies on the bed, he lowers his over mine and kisses me. It's a deep, ravenous kiss but there's nothing rough about it.

His mouth travels lower, kissing down my neck and chest until he claims one of my hard nipples, licking and teasing before he draws it into his mouth and begins to suck. I sink my fingers into his hair, letting the tips of my nails graze his scalp.

He releases my nipple, and presses his hands against the mattress to lift his upper body. His strokes become longer and harder, his breathing shallower and louder, his muscles tenser and tighter until his strokes shorten and his breath comes in quick moans that ratchet up an octave. His eye lock onto mine until he loses control and has to squeeze them shut, waiting for his body to relax.

I stare up at him and know whatever is happening between us is burning too bright, too fast, but it feels too damn good to care about what may come.

"Give me five minutes to recover," he says, trying to steady his breathing.

"I can't go another round. I need to be able to walk tomorrow. And don't you dare smile about that."

He laughs. "You didn't let me finish. Give me five minutes, and then I'll get dressed and take you to lunch."

"I already made lunch, but I haven't had a chance to eat it."

"Put it in the fridge. Eat it for dinner."

"What if someone sees us together?"

"We won't go anywhere close. And if someone sees us, we're just two coworkers having lunch."

"What about leaving the building together?"

"Shit. I hate having to act like a damn kid sneaking out of the house, but yeah, I guess we should probably walk out separately."

"We should take our own cars, too. If someone sees us both getting into the same—"

"Fuck that. No. I'm a grown man and I want to take you to lunch, not *meet* you for lunch." He leaves my bed and walks toward the bathroom. "I'm taking you to lunch."

I stop to grab my charcuterie from Gran's desk so I can put it in the fridge. Vaughn takes one look at the plate and says, "Please tell me that's not what you were calling lunch."

"This is a perfectly fine lunch."

"That's a snack. It's a good thing I came over."

"You only came over because I asked to borrow a ladder."

He smiles like I've said something adorable. "I would've come over to give you the flowers, Landry."

Right. My first flowers.

By the time we step into the parking garage together, I no longer care about being seen with him. But somehow, I care a lot more about how he sees me.

HER HANDS ARE FLAWLESS—LONG, elegant fingers, perfectly shaped fingernails. I can't help but watch them every time she takes a tortilla chip and drags it through the guacamole, and brings it to her pretty mouth.

My brain jumped from "she's too young" to being mesmerized by watching her eat fucking chips and guac in the span of week. I'm pumping the mental brakes as hard as I can, but I've already compiled a cache of memories that are keeping my engine revved, regardless. I look down at my own scarred, dry hands and wonder why she ever let me put them on her smooth, soft body to begin with.

She talks with her hands, too, and she's constantly talking, so they're always moving, dragging my eyes with them. I don't know what kind of guy she should date, but I know it sure as shit shouldn't be me.

A waiter walks by, carrying a tray full of fish-bowl-sized margaritas, and her eyes follow him. I bristle internally, until I realize she's looking at the drinks, not the waiter's arms and shoulders. Mostly the drinks, anyway. "Looks like somebody's having a celebratory lunch," she said.

"We can day drink if you want to blow off the rest of your unpacking."

"How about we stop at the liquor store on the way home, and I'll make us way better margaritas?"

"You're pretty confident in your bartending skills."

"Have you been disappointed in any of my skills so far?"

I desperately want to have a witty comeback for that, but the sudden tightness at my zipper throws off my timing.

Our plates arrive, and my eyes go to her hand as she picks up her fork and cuts into her enchiladas. She takes the first bite and dramatically rolls her eyes back like it's the best thing she's ever tasted. *Fuuuuck me.*

The food is good, but being able to catch that image of her reaction would have been worth it even if this had turned out to be the worst Mexican food in the city.

She tries to pay again, just like she did with the damn pizza. "Hey, if I offer to order food or invite you out to eat, you can always assume I plan on paying, okay?"

"I appreciate that, but you can always assume I'm willing to pay my own way."

"Noted. But you can keep your wallet in your purse from now on."

"Unless it's my idea to go eat. Then I can pay for both of us."

Stubborn to a fault, I swear. "Let's burn that bridge when we come to it. Today, it was my idea, so I'm paying the bill."

"Caveman."

"Ball buster."

"Put that on my tombstone."

The pen slips as I'm trying to sign my name on the ticket. It's hard to write and laugh at the same time. My signature looks like it was scribbled by a toddler. Eh, good enough. "You know I have high expectations for these margaritas, right?"

"Oh, they will surpass your expectations." She slips out of the booth and runs her hands over the back of her shorts to smooth the fabric. My palms itch to give them a second pass, but I'm not actually stupid enough to touch her ass in public. Besides, punching me in the mouth would take an unfair toll on her perfect fingers.

With a quick glance over her shoulder, she says, "In the interest of avoiding an argument at the liquor store, I'm telling you now, you can keep your wallet in your pocket."

Now I want to put a hand on her ass in a whole other way. I'm definitely not stupid enough to do that here, but I'm filing it away for later. She doesn't know she's accumulating brat points. Or does she? I can't actually tell yet. Maybe she doesn't know yet either. The thought of being the one who helps her unlock her kinks, or even one new kink, has my cock straining against my zipper again. *Sure, let's add tequila to the equation. My brakes have already fucking failed, anyway.*

I reach to take the bags from Landry as she comes around the back of my truck in the parking garage. I let her buy the damn liquor, but she's not carrying the bags in while I walk next to her with an empty hand. I had to step in front of her at the grocery store to keep her from paying for the salt and limes, too. And the melon. I would've never guessed we'd need watermelon for margaritas.

"You're already carrying the melon," she objects. "If you drop it, you'll never know the orgasmic wonder of my watermelon 'ritas."

"I can carry the orgasmic melon and the bags." I open and close my hand impatiently, keeping the melon cradled in my opposite arm. "Give them to me."

She holds the loops open so I can grab them. "Fine. But if you drop that watermelon, I'm having one delivered."

"Is it still orgasmic if you don't pick it out yourself?"

"If you drop that one, you better hope so. I've got my heart set on these margaritas and I'm not in the mood to compromise."

If I hadn't already known she wasn't big on compromise, her brand of tequila and the fact that she insisted on buying Grand Marnier and habanero bitters to also go in these fancy-ass drinks left no doubt. She drinks like a girl. A girl with high standards. And a high tolerance for spice, apparently.

I hold the door open at the top of the stairs and motion for her to walk through ahead of me. Southern boy manners are hardwired. And I'm hardwired to want to feel her body brush against mine as she maneuvers past me in the doorway. Chivalry ain't dead, but neither is my dick.

A familiar voice throws ice water on my yearning. "Well, would you look at that, Lolly Girl." Vonnie smiles and nuzzles Lolita's head against her cheek. What the hell is she doing on the eighth floor? Besides spying. She probably roams every hallway, trolling for gossip. Landry freezes, stays rooted to the carpet even after I let the door close behind me when I step into the hallway. "If that's not the epitome of a gentleman. Carrying a woman's groceries. Be still my heart."

Landry forces a smile. "I pulled in at the perfect moment. Must be my lucky day."

Vonnie's sharp eyes cut to the exuberant rabbit logo on the bags dangling from my hand. "Oh, and you went to Spec's, too. Stocking your liquor cabinet, huh? Well, good for you, honey." She winks at Landry.

"Just a few essentials." Landry's voice trails like she might say more.

So help me, if she invites Vonnie to have a drink with us, I will drop this watermelon right here.

"You don't have to explain anything to me." The snake's tongue darts out, and her owner's eyes dart between Landry and me. "Don't let me keep you. I was just up here, finishing off my afternoon walk. It's getting too hot to walk outside. Can't take the heat so much these days. You'll see me making my rounds in the halls until it cools off again."

Great. Fucking great. Of course, we will. For the next five months, I guess.

"Have a good evening," Landry says.

"You do the same, darlin'." Vonnie sashays off toward the elevators, humming that damn song she keeps inserting my name into.

Her serenade follows us down the hall. "At laaaaaaaast, my Vawwwwn has come along . . ." The ding of the elevator has never sounded so sweet.

Landry

WE MAKE IT INSIDE my apartment with the melon and all the bottles still intact, but I completely lose my composure as soon as the door is shut behind us. My laughter borders on hysterical. Vaughn grunts as he walks past me. He sets everything on the kitchen counter.

"Seems like Vonnie's changed her mind about you," he says. "Since when are y'all on such friendly terms?"

"I hung around after work one day and had a glass of wine with her and Carina. She told some stories, and I started to understand her a little better." I dig my blender out of a box. "But hey, I'm not the one she wrote a song for."

"She did not write that song. She just added my name to it."

I plug in the blender, take the cutting board from the drain rack, and point at a drawer. "Can you hand me a knife from in there?"

"Use this one," Vaughn says, pulling the knife I'd used to cut up cheese earlier from the drain rack.

"You can cut the limes with that one. I need a big one for the watermelon."

"I'll cut the watermelon."

"Why? Because you're the man you should get to use the bigger knife?"

"Do you have to turn everything into a debate?"

"All I did was ask for a knife. You're the one who argued."

"Fine." He opens the drawer and pulls out the biggest knife I own.

"Thank you." I set the melon on the cutting board and slice off one end, spin it around and slice off the other. After I stand it upright, I begin to shear off the sides of the rind. On the third slice down the side, my hand slips and the blade catches the middle knuckle on my thumb. "Ouch!"

Vaughn drops the paring knife he's using into the sink and grabs my hand. "Did you cut yourself? Let me see."

"It's nothing. I'm fine."

"Now I'm going to be the reason you have a scar on your perfect hand. Because I let you use that knife."

"You let me? It's my knife. I can use it whenever I want. But this isn't going to leave a scar. It's a teeny, tiny little nick."

"I just meant it wouldn't have happened if I'd been cutting the watermelon." I flinch when he rubs his thumb over it. "See, it's not nothing," he scolds. "You're hurt."

"It hurts because you're getting lime juice in it. Let go."

He lets go and washes his hands, drying them on a paper towel as he shakes his head at me. "Do you have band-aids?"

"Somewhere in a box in one of the bathrooms, but I don't need one. It's barely even bleeding." I apply pressure with the one kitchen towel I've unpacked. It's not deep; it's just that fingers bleed and sting, even from a paper cut.

"Goddammit, Landry." He storms across the room and opens my front door. "I'll be right back."

Honestly, it's probably better if he gets me a bandage from his place. I'm pretty sure all I have are the ones with neon frogs showing peace signs. They're cute, but they don't exactly exude big knife energy.

I finish taking the rind off the watermelon and start cutting it into chunks and putting them in the blender. By the time he comes back, I have the melon pureeing and the limes all halved.

He hasn't calmed down by much, and he gives me a mean look when sees that I've finished all the cutting. I dry my hands and let him put the bandage on my thumb. He's so gentle, like my hand might break in his. When he's done, he kisses it. "I'm sorry I got mad. I didn't mean to treat you like you were incompetent. I just didn't want you to get hurt."

"You're supposed to kiss it before you put the band-aid on."

He manages not to laugh but I almost got him. "I'll kiss it whenever the fuck I want."

"You think so, huh?"

"Where's my margarita?"

"The cocktail shaker should be in the box that says high up right sink."

"What?"

I point up and to the right of the sink. "That's where I'm going to put my bar supplies, in that high cabinet up there to the right."

"Dear God, you should come with an interpreter."

"I just interpreted it for you. Do you want a drink or not?"

He finds the box and opens the flaps. After a few seconds of rummaging around, he says, "You have got to be fucking kidding me."

"Thanks!" I step over and take the shaker from him, not bothering to ask for clarification. "I like a little bling sometimes."

"How do you wash that thing?"

"With soap and water."

"The beads don't come off?"

"They're rhinestones, and no, they don't come off."

"How are you the same girl who drank beers with me on the roof?"

"Beer? Gross. That must've been my twin. Wait a minute! Are you sleeping with both of us?" It's becoming my favorite thing when he has to work so hard not to laugh. "Sometimes, I'm a beer girl. Sometimes, wine." I waggle my blinged-out shaker between us. "And sometimes, I need to mix up some orgasmic watermelon 'ritas."

"You keep using that word."

"You'll see."

He squeezes the juice from the limes to protect me from the sting of it seeping into my cut. I'm happy to let him take over that task.

I shake up the second margarita and pour it into the waiting salt-rimmed glass. Vaughn can't resist pointing out the fact that I unpacked my margarita glasses before my bandages, and questioning what that says about my priorities. I finish our drinks with a lime wedge and drops of habanero bitters.

"Shouldn't you have added the bitters to the shaker?"

"No, it's better like this."

"Did you count how many drops of that stuff you used?"

"Nope. I don't need to. It's the right amount." I lift a glass, and he takes the other. "Trust me." I wink, and clink my glass to his. "Cheers."

He takes his first sip and pretends to be unsure if he likes it or not. He likes it. I can tell. After the second sip, he coughs a little. "So, when does the orgasm hit?"

I shrug. "After we finish these and I suck your dick?"

That sends him into a full choking fit.

"Careful. Those spicy bitters can be a lot when they hit the back of your throat."

"Did you do a couple shots while I was across the hall?"

"I just don't want you to leave disappointed in my bartending skills."

"Nothing about you is disappointing. Infuriating, yes, but never disappointing."

"You haven't known me long enough to say never."

"I definitely haven't known you long enough."

"Well, I live here now, so you're stuck with me. Cheers, neighbor."

"Cheers."

Neither one of us even bothers pretending we didn't intend for him to still be in my bed when we wake up Sunday morning. He's looking at me when I open my eyes. "Don't watch me sleep. That's weird."

"I just opened my own eyes. I wasn't watching you."

Pretty sure he's lying. Positive I don't care. "Thanks for helping me put the rest of my books on the shelves. And the other stuff."

"You're welcome. Thanks for the orgasmic margaritas."

"Told you they'd lead to orgasms."

He laughs. "I'd offer you one more but I promised a buddy I'd help him demo a bathroom he's remodeling."

"Do you always help other people work on your day off?"

"Not always."

"I've got to get back in the gym today. Want some green juice for the road? It'll give you energy."

"No, thanks. I'll stick to coffee." He pulls his jeans up and buttons them. The way they fit so snugly at his waist, bisecting the V of his toned obliques, has my gaze drifting downward, actively appreciating the memory of everything that lies beneath that denim hug. Who knew watching a man put his clothes back on could be so sexy? He pulls his t-shirt down and hides all his defined abs from me, which is good because I'm not sure I'd have ever stopped mapping their definition with my eyes if he hadn't blocked the view.

Show's over. Time to get up and face the consequences of my own actions—specifically, taking way too many days off from the gym. I'mgoing to pay for that break, I'm sure. Maybe Vaughn will help me work out my soreness later, or take advantage of my weakened state. I smile, still lying naked between my sheets—until a pillow hits my face.

"Get up, lazy. You've got boxes to unpack." He plants a goodbye kiss on my forehead. "I'm taking the ladder so I don't have to worry about you hurting yourself."

"Are you going to take all my knives, too?"

"Don't tempt me."

"Watch out for Vonnie."

"I'll make sure the coast is clear. Have a good workout."

I wait until I hear my front door close behind him before I force myself to get up.

My green juice turns gray after I add blueberries to the blender. It doesn't look appetizing but it tastes great, and I need it. I'm not hungover but I'm probably dehydrated from the alcohol. And sluggish from all the carbs and grease I've consumed lately. And weak from fraternizing with the hottest maintenance man alive . . . I should probably stock up on ingredients for green juice.

Vaughn

I STAND UNDER THE shower head and let the hot water soothe my aching shoulders and sore back muscles. That bathroom demo was a bitch. I crank up the hot water and turn my shower into a sauna. For the first time in days, Landry doesn't infiltrate my shower thoughts. Not that I even have the energy for that right now. Breathing all this steam is going to steal the last ounce of strength I have, but that's fine because all I want to do after I get out is crash.

As soon as I pull on a pair of shorts, my phone lights up. It's the after-hours maintenance number. *Fuuuuck me.*

Letting it go to voicemail is an option, but then I'll still have to listen to it. It's Autry McDaniel, one of the original two tenants here. His voice is panicked and he's not speaking in complete sentences, but I catch enough to know there's water coming through his bathroom ceiling. He follows with some barely coherent words about "that harlot upstairs" . . . irresponsible, probably drunk, maybe drowned in her bathtub, should he call 9-1-1?

The harlot upstairs is in unit 501, the woman who likes to answer her door wearing lingerie. It's no secret she loves attention, but I can't imagine she'd flood her own bathroom for it. "I'm on my way. I'll go to her unit first and see if I can get her to come to the door. Don't call 9-1-1 yet. Sit tight."

"Hurry!"

501 answers her door right away. She's wearing leggings and a t-shirt, so it seems unlikely she's pulling a stunt for attention. "Is there water running in your bathroom?"

"No, but if that's all it takes to get you to come running, I'll be sure and turn it on more often."

"The tenant right below you on fourth floor has water coming through his bathroom ceiling, and I'm trying to find the source. Do you mind if I come in and take a quick look?"

There's no sign of a leak in her bathroom. I stop to look in the kitchen before I leave, just to be sure. She follows me from room to room. "Our new manager sure is a pretty young thing."

"She's very pretty." I get on all fours to look under her kitchen sink. She steps closer to me until her leg is practically rubbing against my shoulder.

"And young," she adds.

Thanks for the reminder. "Yeah, that, too." I stand up, careful to pivot to the side as I rise to avoid coming face-to-face with her crotch.

"Okay, everything looks good here. Thanks."

"Glad you liked what you saw." She winks.

I practically jog for the door. Yes, I'm anxious to get out of her apartment, but if Autry's got water gushing through his ceiling, I need to get down there and get it stopped as soon as I can. And if it's not coming from this unit, it's obviously not going to be an easy fix.

Autry is waiting for me in his doorway. "Is she alive up there?"

"Everything's fine upstairs." I enter his unit and go straight to bathroom. What. The. Hell?

He shows up in this doorway now. "Well, where do you think it's coming from?"

He's an old man. Deep breaths. "Is this the emergency?" I point straight up at the fresh, barely visible water spot on the ceiling. Granted, there is definitely moisture up there, and that does indicate a leak somewhere, but there is not a waterfall in his bathroom like he made it out to be on the phone.

"That wasn't there earlier today. It happened fast, I'm telling you. The ceiling will fall if too much water accumulates up there!"

"I know." I run my hand through my hair and try not to lose my patience. "But I promise your ceiling is a long way from falling. I'll look into it tomorrow morning. There's no imminent threat. You can rest easy tonight."

"But you're already here. Why not just track it down now?"

"I am incredibly tired right now. Trust me, I'll do a much better job tomorrow than I would tonight."

"Why are you so tired? Are you not sleeping well? Have you tried melatonin because I tell you what—"

"It's been a busy weekend. I helped a friend start a bathroom remodel, helped someone move—"

"It wasn't by any chance *young* Miss Landry you helped move, was it?"

His emphasis on the word young pisses me off. Doesn't anybody notice anything else about her? She's not just young. And it's not like I'm fucking ancient. "Technically, I just helped her unpack some things. Being a good neighbor."

"Do you think it's wise for the two of you to live right across the hall from one another?"

"I think it's perfectly fine." I don't mean to snap, but he needs to stop.

"I'm just pointing out the obvious temptation. I was a young man once myself, you know?"

Oh, so now I'm young, too, huh? "I honestly don't foresee any problems with that."

"Okay, well, I do hope you get some sleep tonight. I trust I'll see you bright and early tomorrow morning?"

"My version of bright and early is about eight."

"Perfect. I'll have already had my oatmeal and my morning walk by then."

It occurs to me he probably walks in the mornings to avoid running into Vonnie on her evening walks. There has to be some history there. I wonder if they were neighbors with benefits, or more, at some point. They've lived here for forty years, and it's hard to believe a man and woman could despise each other as much as they do without having been fond of each other at some point. "See you in the morning."

All I can think about on the way back to my apartment is what will happen if things go south between me and Landry. What if she ends up hating me? There's no way we could both keep working here. Or living here. I should've never touched her. She's undeniably young and pretty, as noted by everyone in the whole goddamn building, but she's so much more. Funny. Kind. Interesting. Genuinely independent. Hell, everything about her seems genuine. And she's so easy to be around. Easy to talk to, laugh with . . . she makes it easy for me to just be.

That should scare the hell out of me, but I don't remember the last time I felt like I could let go like I can with her. I want to let go of so damn much. I want to just fucking be.

Especially when I'm with her.

Landry

Gah! Why are Monday alarms the loudest?

I groan and haphazardly poke at my phone until it shuts up. But when I roll over and see the sunlight streaming in, hear the distant sounds of construction happening on the street below, and smell the faint lemon pound cake scent of the unlit candle on my nightstand, I sit straight up and breathe it all in.

No asshole is going to cut me off in traffic this morning, no wreck will have me stuck on the freeway, worrying about whether or not I'm going to be late, and no exhaust fumes will sneak in through my air vents and try to choke me. My commute is now nothing more than an eight-floor elevator ride. I flop back onto my mattress and smile.

I love this apartment. I like my job, my coworkers—one of them a whole lot more than I should. Vaughn is the most unexpected part of it all. It seems like it's been months since he shook that uniform shirt in my face and tried to let me know what was what. It's a good thing he's hot. And funny. And sweet. Even if he is also grumpy, impatient, and bossy as hell. Okay, I don't entirely mind the dominant part.

How did we jump from day one to here so damn fast? Rhetorical question, obviously. All I have to do is look at him, or envision him, and I know exactly how it happened. I remember every second of it in explicit detail. Day one was a shock, but night one . . . that was what poured the gasoline on the fire.

What's the worst that could happen if it burns out just as quickly? Awkwardness. Unemployment. Homelessness. Shit, I've got to get out of this bed. Like Carina said, I can't blame traffic if I'm late. And I'm not doing myself any favors, lying here going over what-ifs that might never happen.

Anything can happen, but anything can not happen, too.

The best part of not having a commute is that I can use the gym before work. I could sleep a little more, but the workout is a better choice.

My ponytail is high, my water bottle is full, and I'm ready to sweat. I close my door carefully, a habit I developed to keep from waking my neighbor in my old place. She was retired and reminded me of my grandma, and she probably got up hours before me, but I still worried about waking her. As soon as the lock snicks at the turn of my key, Vaughn's door opens behind me.

Oh, sweet, sexy, short-haired, shirtless Jesus! He's already sweaty.

"Do you run?" he asks, nodding at my shoes. There's a hopeful lilt to his voice.

"Not unless I'm being chased." I laugh.

His eyebrows lift, and his smirk causes me to avert my eyes. I know he can't look into my irises and read my mind, but reflexes do what reflexes do.

"You look like you already got your morning workout in," I tease.

"Sometimes, the treadmill won't cut it. I need to feel hard ground under my feet, you know?"

"I wish I did. I hear that runner's high is pretty incredible."

"You could come with me and find out."

"If I come with you, all I'll find out is that I can't keep up. Not to mention, I'll probably puke, and I try really hard not to puke in front of a guy until I've known him for at least a month."

He looks taken aback for a few seconds. "Wow, I know it hasn't actually been a month since we met, but hearing you say it out loud sounds crazy." We start down the hall together.

"Well, at least now you know what you've got to look forward to when we hit the one-month mark."

His deep laugh almost makes me reconsider running with him. Almost.

The elevator is empty when the doors open. When they shut, the air feels like we've stepped into a lightning storm. Sizzling. Perilous. Highly charged. A tenant on the fifth floor intrudes on our private space and neutralizes it instantly. Two more people get on when we reach the third floor and one on the second. We all file out into the lobby.

"Enjoy your run."

"Last chance," he says, cutting his eyes to the glass doors. It's a gorgeous blue-sky morning, but I'm not a runner. I shake my head and hook my thumb over my shoulder toward the gym. His smile is enticing, but it makes me want to kiss him, not run with him. "I don't know what you've got against fresh air, but okay, I guess."

I start to walk away as he heads out the door, but I pause and watch him jog off down the sidewalk. The desire to run after him twinges like a stitch in my side, not strong enough to make me do it, but a little sharper than I'm ready to feel.

Our hallway is empty when I get back from the gym. Staring at his door, I wonder if he's back from his run. I let myself into my apartment before my imagination gets carried away.

Carina already has coffee going when I walk into the office. She's bright-eyed as always. "Good morning. How was the commute?"

"Brutal. The elevator stopped twice on the way down."

"Glad you showed up with a sense of humor. I have a feeling we're going to need it today."

"Why?"

"Full moon."

"Do you really believe that makes people more dramatic than usual?"

"It does. You've honestly never noticed?"

"I don't really keep up with the phases of the moon, so I can't honestly say."

"I'll keep you updated from now on. You'll see the effects."

"I'll try to keep an open mind."

"I'll open it for you. Don't worry." She holds out a small, floral gift bag.

"What's this?"

"A housewarming gift."

"Carina, that's so sweet." Under the layers of pastel tissue paper, I find a cotton drawstring pouch. I let its contents tumble onto my palm. There are five rough multicolored stones and a card that says *Housewarming Crystals*.

"I almost got you the polished set, but something told me you might like the raw crystals better."

"Is it offensive to call them pretty?" I wince because I really don't want to offend her, but I know nothing about crystals.

"Not at all. But they're more than pretty. The card explains their purposes. There's a bowl in there, too."

I remove more tissue paper and find a small white bowl that's carved from some other kind of stone. Again, I have no idea what I'm looking at, but it's pretty. "Thank you. Is there a specific place I'm supposed to put them?"

"That set is particularly good for a living room or an office, anywhere you want protection but also energy and clarity. They work well together so you can keep them all in that bowl. It's selenite to charge them."

I've spent my whole life thinking crystals were nothing more than pretty rocks and that people who believed anything else were delusional, but Carina's so sincere, and she's one of the nicest people ever, so I wouldn't dare say anything dismissive about this gift. "Maybe we can close the office for a little while at lunch and go upstairs. You can see my apartment and help me decide where to put them."

"I'd love that!"

For the time being, I place the crystals in their charging bowl and set it on my desk. This Monday is off to a great start, full moon or not.

Our good vibes are splintered by a flustered tenant who barges in holding a plastic cup at arms-length. There is a paper towel over the top and it's held in place by a rubber band around the rim. "I found this in my apartment!" she shrieks. "Do we not have pest control here?"

My stomach flips at the thought of what she might've captured in that cup. There is no way in hell I'm taking that rubber band off, and if she reaches for it, I swear I'll pelt her in the forehead with crystals. They'll be good for protection all right.

"What is it?" I ask.

"A tarantula, that's what it is!"

I pull my legs up into my chair, as if my feet being on the ground put me in greater danger, when what I should be doing is keeping them firmly planted, preparing to run.

"Oh, it won't hurt you," Carina says. "You can leave it here. I'll take it outside and let it go."

"So it can crawl right back in?" The woman is mortified by Carina's suggestion.

"I won't put it near the door. I'll take it to the edge of the lawn."

That seems to ease the woman's fears. "Okay, here." She sets the cup on Carina's desk and backs away from it. "But you need to call an exterminator before we're overrun with those things."

"Tarantulas are part of nature's pest control," Carina says. "We don't want to wipe them out because they eat insects that are harmful to gardens. What would you rather have, a few basically harmless tarantulas or a decimated garden?"

I lock eyes with the frightened tenant, who I've yet to meet, but I know we both care less about this hypothetical garden than Carina does. Before either of us can answer the question, the cup begins to hiss. Even Carina's eyes go wide, and she scoots her chair away from her desk a few feet. "They make that sound when they feel threatened," she says. "It can't get out though. And even if it did, it wouldn't hurt us. It would just run away."

The cup wobbles, and then it topples, and begins to roll across her desk toward her. We all scream. Okay, only the woman who provided the cup-o-spider and I scream, but even Carina lets out a quick yip and backs away from her desk.

Vaughn and Holden rush into the office. I didn't know they were down here, but I'm glad to see them. Pointing at the cup, I say, "There's a tarantula in there. She caught it." I shift my pointing finger toward the tenant.

The cup has stopped rolling near the edge of Carina's desk. The hissing has also stopped. The rubber band and paper towel are still securely in place. Holden steps toward it. "Tarantulas won't hurt you. They won't even spit the stinging hair at you unless you get close and scare them."

"They spit hair?" If that was meant to allay my fears, it had the exact opposite effect.

"Only if they feel threatened." He picks up the cup as if it doesn't contain a hissing, hair-spitting eight-legged nightmare. "It's not really hair, more similar to fiberglass."

"Oh, that's much better," I say.

Vaughn has his hand over his mouth, but it doesn't block the sound of his laughter. Carina laughs a little now, too. "Holden's right," she says. "But even I freaked out when that cup started rolling in my direction."

She, Holden, and Vaughn appear to be sharing a bonding moment as they laugh at the supposed silliness of being afraid of a tarantula. The spidernapper and I share our own bonding moment, replete with horrified glances and full body shudders, entirely devoid of laughter.

I hate that I'm such a stereotype of girliness when it comes to the creepy crawlies, but I can't help it. I don't even like ladybugs. They're cute to look at but I don't want to hold one. Dragonflies are cool from a distance. Butterflies? Beautiful. But if one landed on me, I'd probably lose my shit. It's those spindly legs—irrational or not, no, thank you. "Can you take it outside?" I say to Holden. "It probably needs some air."

He nods and walks out with the cup. Vaughn asks if I'm okay.

"Yeah, I'm good." I'd be better if he could hug me right now, but we both know he can't. I want to believe that look in his eyes is because he wants to, though.

"Hi," I say to the tenant who provided this morning's adrenaline rush. "I'm Landry Channing, the new manager and fellow arachnophobe."

She extends her hand. "Hi, I'm Delaney Mitchell. I live in 611. Sorry to turn the morning into a horror flick, but when I saw that thing in my kitchen, just staring at me . . ." She shudders again, and then she turns to Vaughn. "Can you come look in my apartment and make sure there's not a whole nest of them somewhere?"

He looks like he's about to blow her off. I beam a *be nice* message from my eyes to his. Fortunately, he gets it. "It's unlikely you've got any more. You probably carried it inside in a bag or a box and didn't even realize it." She looks like she might be sick at the thought, so he quickly adds, "I'm busy this morning, trying to track down a water leak, but I'll come up later and take a look around, okay?"

"Can you at least walk me back inside so I can grab my purse? I was on my way to work but I'm afraid to go back in my apartment alone."

Huh, she wasn't too afraid to trap a tarantula, but now she can't go back into her apartment without Vaughn to protect her?

I remind myself I don't do jealousy. Where did that petty thought even come from?

Holden bounces back into the office. "That wasn't a tarantula. It was a wolf spider."

"Do they spit fiberglass?" I ask.

"No, and they won't bite unless they feel threatened, same as the tarantula. Wolf spiders are wicked fast though." He uses his fingers to mime an airborne running spider. "And they pounce on their prey." His hand rises and falls quickly to illustrate that trait as well. My whole body convulses. "And they have great eyesight. Some of their eyes have reflective tissue, so if you shine a flashlight on them, they glow."

"Please stop talking."

Delaney has stepped closer to Vaughn, just like I did when Lolita slithered onto the scene my first day here. Well, not just like that. I mean, her boobs don't appear to have made contact with his arm. "Holden seems to be our resident spider expert," I say. "Maybe he should take you back to your apartment to make sure you don't have any more uninvited hairy guests."

"I don't care who does it," she says. "I just want to know someone has checked every nook and cranny."

"Holden, do you mind inspecting all Delaney's nooks and crannies?" *Ooooh, that did not sound right.*

"Um, not at all." The two of them leave the office. Delaney turns back and mouths a thank you to me. I guess she really didn't care who acted as spider patrol.

I can feel Vaughn's eyes on me.

"What? I thought you probably wanted to get back to tracking down that leak you mentioned, and I figured it was better to have Holden take care of the spider search. If you're just dying to check her nooks and crannies, too, I'm sure you can still go up later like you promised. I didn't mean to speak for you. She'd probably appreciate a second set of eyes." I'm rambling.

"I'm sure Holden will do a thorough job. He'd be thrilled to find a spider."

"Exactly. That's why I said he should go."

"Right."

"Right. And you should go find that water leak."

"On my way."

"Where is the leak, by the way?"

"Don't know yet. That's why I'm looking for it. But there's a water mark on Autry McDaniel's bathroom ceiling."

"You could've just said it was in his apartment."

"The leak isn't in his apartment. Just the evidence of it is."

"Well, go find out where it is then."

"I'm trying."

"By staring at me? I'm not the leak."

"Good to know. I'll mark you off the list." He doesn't put his hand over his mouth this time, just laughs out loud as he leaves.

I turn to find Carina staring at me. "What?"

"Do you want to go to a yoga class with me tonight?"

"I already told you I don't do yoga."

"Yeah, I know. But I really think you should."

We make it to lunch with no more excitement. Looks like we've tapped out the full moon's drama.

The Fed-Ex guy does mention the cool spider in the planter by the front door, but I choose to believe it's not the wolf spider Holden took outside. Surely, he didn't put it in a pot right by the front door. Of course, I didn't specifically tell him not to, so he probably did. "Whatever spider he's talking about would prefer living outside and wouldn't risk coming back inside, right?"

Carina agrees, but it's not lost on me that she might be agreeing just to keep me calm. She's big on calm. I would like to be bigger on it myself but every time calm and I get too close, things go haywire.

By noon, I'm feeling stir crazy. I need to get out of the office. "I have charcuterie items in my fridge. Wanna go up and help me eat them?" I lift the little bowl of crystals. "And help me find the best spot for these?"

"Absolutely."

We hang the *"Out on Property. Be Back Soon"* sign on the office door and make our escape. I do like my job, but some days sitting at a desk for too long starts to feel suffocating. The hectic days are better, but today, calm has followed the spider.

Carina's eyes zero in on the flowers on my counter the moment she steps inside. "Those are gorgeous."

"Thanks," I say, dropping my purse on the table inside my door. "They're from Vaughn." *Shit. I probably shouldn't have told her that.*

"Ohhhhhh, I see."

"They're housewarming flowers. You gave me a housewarming gift."

"Yeah, I'm sure it's exactly the same." She laughs, but it's light-hearted.

She and I agree the crystals look great on the entry table. Carina says they'll probably function well there. I trust her. There's a thin groove along the back edge of the small table that works great to prop up the card explaining the crystals. "If I leave this here, I'll eventually remember what each one is and what it's does."

Carina smiles. "I have a book I can loan you that explains a lot more, if you like reading about stuff like that."

"I love books in general. Wanna see my library?"

"Is that a real question? Hell, yeah, I want to see your library."

I flip the light on and step aside so she can enter my favorite room. "Holy shit! Those bookshelves are amazing. I didn't even know the last manager liked books."

"Oh, they weren't here before. Vaughn built them for me." *Shit. Stop doing that.*

"Did you two know each other before you came to work here?"

"No. You witnessed our first meeting, when he shoved that shirt in my face in a magenta rage." I laugh.

"Huh. You just asked him to build these and he did?"

"He said he couldn't at first, but then he surprised me."

"These must've taken some time."

"He built them in a day, but I'm not sure he got anything else done that day. And I think he may have stayed up all night painting them so they'd be ready when I moved in. I offered to help him paint, but he wouldn't let me."

Her eyes keep getting bigger the more information I spew.

"I asked for a ladder on a rail, but he said no to that." I rush the words out like they're some sort of proof he wasn't giving me special treatment. Never mind that everything I've already said before this is a firm indictment to the contrary.

"Maybe you should ask again. I have a feeling his ability to say no to you isn't all that strong."

"Well, anyway, if I forget to return your book on crystals, you'll know where to find it. We should eat." I turn off the light and leave the room.

She definitely suspected things when Vaughn and I tripped over our words about my missing key, but I've erased any possible doubt that could've remained. Carina's cool, though. It probably wouldn't even matter if I told her outright, which I won't.

Damn, I can never have drinks with her. I think I might be desperate for a friend to share all my dirty secrets with. It's been too long since I've had that in my life, but I'm her boss. She's not looking to be my bestie.

I'm technically Vaughn's boss, too. I am the worst property manager ever. Screw the maintenance guy, overshare with the leasing agent . . . I don't even know how to interact with people anymore. Not responsibly, anyway.

Carina doesn't mention Vaughn again. We finish off all my cheese, prosciutto, and grapes. I'm happy to share it with her. It would've probably gone bad before I ate it all. "I have some hummus and mini pita bread, too."

"Bring it on. I love hummus."

"Me, too." She's fun. It's a shame we can't become real friends.

I admire the little bowl full of colorful stones on our way out. There's something comforting about them, and a part of me wants to believe they can do the things listed on the card behind them. What's the saying . . . wanting to believe is halfway to believing? It's a famous quote, I think.

When we step off the elevator, Vaughn calls out, "Hey, Landry. Can I talk to you for a minute?"

"Yeah, sure." He can't possibly know I told Carina he gave me flowers, or what I told her about the bookshelves. Can he? His tone sounds agitated.

"See you back in the office," Carina says.

I go to Vaughn with my head held high. "What's up?"

He grabs my wrists and pulls me forward. "What the hell?" I sputter.

Without answering, he shoves me into an electrical closet, follows me inside, and closes the door. It's pitch dark in here. "Vaughn, what are you doing?"

"I've already tracked down one leak this morning, but I heard you had a wet spot that needed to be investigated, too." His hand slides up my skirt and cups my pussy through my panties. "Oh, yeah, there it is. Don't worry, I promise I'll find the source of the leak." His hand slips underneath the fabric, and his finger slides through my seam a few times before he plunges it inside me.

"We can't do this now." I push against his chest. "And definitely not here."

He nips at the base of my neck, working his way upward, sucking and kissing. He's already added a second finger inside me. "But you're in dire need of maintenance, beautiful. This much wetness indicates you could have a flood any minute. Trust me, I'm a professional."

No lies detected. I rock against his rough hand until the promised flood arrives, which isn't long. I still can't see him at all. "Told you I could help. Unfortunately, there's no permanent fix. We just have to continually release the pressure when it builds up." He whispers against my skin, but his voice is so heavy, so laden with lust that it fills this small space. "But that's what I'm here for. It's part of my job, and I can be of service anytime, anywhere. All you have to do is call."

This was the absolute hottest and most spontaneous thing I've ever experienced. My purse is still on my shoulder. And now we have to open the door and hope no one sees us walking out of a closet together. The risk of getting caught is astronomical. Anyone could be walking through this hallway on their way to the gym, to check their mail, or heading toward the side exit. Every receptor in my body is tingling at the possibility of what lies on the other side of this door. I've never been more turned on in my life.

I'd give anything if we could sneak upstairs now. How am I supposed to work the rest of the day?

Vaughn eases the door open and peeks out. "It's clear. Let's go."

I step out behind him, and he immediately turns in the opposite direction from the office and walks away. That's it? We just go our separate ways as if that scorching encounter didn't just happen? Oh, damn, that makes even hotter.

It takes a couple seconds for my brain to send the message to my feet that they need to move. I straighten my skirt and head for the bathroom.

The woman staring back at me in the mirror is a disheveled mess. I smooth her hair, wipe away her smeared lipstick and reapply it, and smile at her. We have a dirty secret, and we like it.

Vaughn

IT'S BEEN TWO DAYS since I pulled Landry into the electrical closet. I've been getting an early start here so I can knock off early to help Wick with his bathroom remodel, and we've ended up working until it's too late to see her. He usually has contractors on his remodels, but finding an available contractor right now is about as likely as winning the damn lottery.

He's a good friend, lets me use his beach house and his personal trainer discount on workout equipment. My home gym wouldn't be nearly as nice without the benefit of his prices, but every time I get a glimpse of Landry, my dick throbs. The little head is definitely ready to choose her over him. The memory of how fast she came all over my hand when I took her by surprise plays on a constant loop in my head. I'm fucking obsessed.

That wicked little smile she flashes is killing me. There'll be more impromptu sessions in unexpected places. Soon. Tonight should be the last night Wick needs my help. And then I'm all hers—or she's all mine.

I cruise by the office when I take my lunch break, but Landry's out running errands. I'd much rather hide away with her again, but I settle for jerking it to my current favorite memory, and then I go to the pool to get a few laps in before I have to face the next work order.

The sun feels good warming my muscles. I could fall asleep and stay out here until nightfall. That's one of the downsides to living where I work: I can't take a day off and hang out at the pool. Every tenant with an open maintenance request would find me. I head back in to rinse off in the shower, eat a couple sandwiches, and get back to work.

Coffee wouldn't be a bad idea. No sense in making a whole pot, though. There's coffee in the office.

Landry's back at her desk when I walk in. We exchange smiles as I pass her desk on my way to the coffee pot.

"Late night?" she asks.

"I got in a little after midnight. Is there any plain creamer?"

"No," Carina says. "We like vanilla and toffee."

"Fine. I'll drink it black."

Landry spins her chair to face me. "I thought that's how you always drank it."

I raise my eyebrows. She just can't help herself. She's always on the verge of saying too much. "When I make it myself, I drink it black because I buy good coffee. This cheap stuff tastes burnt. It needs creamer."

"All you ever had to do was ask," Carina says. "I'll pick up some plain creamer on my way in tomorrow morning."

"Thanks. This is why you're my favorite."

Landry's spine stiffens, and she leans forward in her chair. "Oh, yeah . . ." she trails off, obviously realizing she has to choose her words carefully. I shouldn't enjoy needling her as much as I do, but she makes it too easy. "If you're going out again tonight," she says, "you could probably pick some up on your way home."

"Oh, it's no problem for me to get it in the morning," Carina offers. "I need to pick up some protein bars, anyway."

Using my back to push the door open, I keep my eyes on Landry as I go, winking when Carina turns away to answer the phone.

She bites her lip and smiles. There's fire in her eyes, and I want to fan the flames, but quick teases are all we can risk. She intentionally baits me as much as I do her. We both love every second of it. I'd forgotten what this level of compatibility felt like. It's addictive.

Wick begs another night of free labor out of me. Apparently, I like to surround myself with people I can't say no to. Also, he offered me his beach house for two full weekends, and the thought of having Landry all to myself at the beach for a whole weekend put me in a giving mood.

I don't regret giving him my Thursday night until I realize she's already got plans for her Friday night. She and another woman are leaving her apartment all dressed up for a girls' night out on the town when I come back from a run.

"Hey," Landry says. "This is Jenna. I'm terrible at keeping in touch, but thankfully, she still talks to me when I finally make an effort. Jenna, this is Vaughn."

"Nice to meet you, Jenna." I can't peel my eyes of Landry in that short black dress. She looks like sugar-coated sin. "Y'all going to a concert?"

"No," Landry says. "Dinner, wine bar, maybe dancing. Wherever the night takes us. And tomorrow and tomorrow night, too. Jenna's staying with me for the whole weekend."

Thanks for that gut punch. "Be safe. You're not driving, are you?"

"We scheduled a ride." Landry glances at her phone. "And he's here. Goodnight!"

"Night." If I'd already had a shower, I might be offering to drive them around for free right now. Might, hell. I'd definitely be offering. Watching Landry's ass as they walk away isn't helping my restraint. *Go inside, you fucking moron.*

Eating pizza alone at my kitchen counter would've been perfectly fine with me a few weeks ago. Tonight, it sucks. All I can think about is other guys watching Landry dance in that dress with her laughter flowing freely, her inhibitions loosened by wine, and the inner rim of her bottom lip stained with it. Goddammit! I either want to fuck or fight.

That's a lie; I only want to do the first one. And only with her.

My empty living room feels pathetic. At least my new couch is coming on Sunday. Maybe Jenna will leave Sunday morning, and Landry will come over and help me break it in. This place will feel more like a home with some furniture in it. I take my beer up to the roof. At least I've got a chair up there.

Sitting alone on the roof, slapping mosquitos off my arms isn't exactly my idea of a great Friday night, but it feels better to be alone up here than in my apartment. I wonder if Landry's told her friend, Jenna, about us. I'm not even sure there is an us. We've haven't thrown our cards on the table and defined anything. It's too early for that, anyway. She might not want an us. Hell, we can't even be an us out in the open, no matter what we want. How much longer is she going to be okay with sneaking around, though?

I smile, thinking about all the shit Wick's given me since I told him about her. Every time he and his girl, Nadine, invite me to something, they always add, "bring a date." And I never do.

It's not that I don't date, but when you start bringing a woman around your friends, it feels like an instant us situation. And I've avoided those for a long time. No us, just me. And dates that don't repeat. Clear expectations, no complications.

Landry's complicated. There are so many reasons why we shouldn't.

My beer's empty, and my veins will be soon if I don't go in and get away from these damn mosquitos.

After taking my second shower of the night, I lie down and flip channels on the TV, stopping on a carpenter building something in his workshop. Cabinets, furniture, I don't know, much less care. It's just background noise to my racing thoughts.

I could spend my weekend building something. Maybe that library ladder Landry wants. But then she wouldn't need me to come over and do pointless shit like put elephants on her top shelves.

Saturday crowds make everything take twice as long—driving, parking, purchasing—which I don't mind so much because it keeps me busy, keeps my mind occupied. Until I get home just in time to see Jenna and Landry leaving her apartment wearing shorts and bikini tops, carrying towels. I'm using one of the property's trolleys to bring up the TV and sound bar I just bought for my living room, and I nearly drop the handle at the sight of Landry in half a bikini. I want to yank down those little shorts so I can see the other half. "Y'all headed to the beach or the pool?"

"The pool," Landry says. "Come hang out with us."

"I might come out later. I've got to install these first."

Both women look at my electronics, and Jenna shakes her head. "Boys and their toys."

"Exactly," I say, laughing. Her face and her tone make me think for sure she knows about Landry and me, and I think my chest may have swelled a little as I realized it. "Have fun."

"Why don't you come have some fun?" Landry asks. "That looks like work. You work all week long."

"Yeah, but this is work for my enjoyment."

"Okay, well, enjoy working on your day off."

"I said I'd come to the pool in a little while."

"No, you said you *might*, and everybody knows might means won't in man-speak."

"It's my experience it means won't in woman-speak."

Jeanna laughs. "Y'all *might* need to get married already."

Landry and I both lose our smiles. Nothing kills a mood faster than the M word, especially when you've already been there, done that. The tension in the air no longer has the playful spark it did a moment ago. Now, it's just tense. Shit, I actually feel bad for Jenna. She wasn't trying to be a buzzkill. "Y'all better get out there and claim pool chairs before they're all taken."

"Yeah," Landry says. "We probably should've gotten up earlier."

I tug on the trolley's handle and bring it closer to my door, making a point not to watch them walk away this time.

Landry

I PRETTY MUCH KNEW Vaughn wouldn't come out to the pool after Jenna commented that we should get married. She was joking, but he didn't find it funny. Neither did I, to be honest. That topic might set me on edge for the rest of my life.

We stayed out late last night, and we're in agreement that we should keep things low-key tonight. Jenna's never had Indian food, and there's no way I'm letting her leave Houston without remedying that. She's the only friend I grew up with who didn't make me out to be the bad guy when I left the golden boy. *Fake-ass motherfucker.* She got a divorce of her own last year, but she's still living in our hometown. I don't think she'll ever leave, but I want to tempt her as much as possible while she's here.

When we head out for dinner, I take my time locking my door, hoping Vaughn might be leaving at the same time. We run into each other in the space between our doors a lot, but not tonight.

After Jenna and I eat our fill of biryani and naan at Aga's, I introduce her to Booza's stretchy ice cream. By the time we get back to my place, we're battling food comas and ready to relax and binge-watch trash TV for the rest of the night.

I catch myself listening for Vaughn's door more than once when I should've been paying attention to what Jenna was saying. He probably won't text me because he knows I have company, but that doesn't stop me from checking my phone in the hopes that he might have. *Might*. Like I don't know what that means.

I promised Jenna brunch, so we're up early Sunday morning to beat the hangover crowd. Again, I stall while locking my door. Vaughn doesn't make an appearance. Lingering outside my door, hoping to see him is pathetic, but I can't help myself.

Jenna's amazed by the lengthy mimosa menu, the coffee choices, and the bloody mary options, including skewers loaded with enough food to be complete meals in themselves. I remember seeing these simple things in that same fascinated way.

They're commonplace to me now, but when you grow up where we did, places like this feel like they're from a whole other world. And they basically are. Plenty of smallish towns have decent options for dining and shopping, but then there are those barren pin-dot places where even Starbucks won't attempt colonization. We're from a pin dot, where you make your coffee at home and you don't drink it over ice. And you damn sure don't need fancy syrups or whipped cream on top. And you double-damn sure don't need champagne with breakfast.

I order a vanilla latte and the tropical mimosa flight.

We hang out in my apartment for a few more hours before Jenna has to hit the road. "It's been so good to catch up with you," I say. "I promise I'll stay in touch this time."

"Me, too. I'm really proud of you, Landry. Your life is cool."

"This better not be the last time you come visit me."

"It won't be."

"You could do it, too, you know? Get out and make a new life anywhere you want. You're single, no kids. There's nothing to stop you."

"My parents depend on me for stuff, and I watch the boys if Chase has to work when it's his weekend to have them."

"Jesus Christ, Jenna! You shouldn't have to plan your life around babysitting your brother's kids and doing shit for your parents. They're not elderly or disabled. I'm sure they're perfectly capable of doing every damn thing they put on you. And Chase can hire a babysitter when he needs one. Those kids are his responsibility, not yours."

"I know, I know. But it's family." She shrugs. "I just feel like that's what you're supposed to do."

Yeah, if you want to be trapped there forever. I take a breath and back off. Making her feel bad about letting her family guilt her into things isn't going to help her situation. And I don't want to push her away when we just got back in touch. "I get it. But if you ever change your mind, you could come to Houston and stay with me until you got your feet on the ground."

"Thanks. I'll keep that in mind." She smiles, and hugs me good-bye. "By the way, I think you should totally go for it with your neighbor. He's into you. I can tell."

"You think so?" More than once this weekend, I almost told her about Vaughn and me, but I kept it to myself. Now, I kind of wish I would've shared it with her.

"Trust me. And keep me posted."

"Deal." It's nice to have one last laugh together before she leaves.

I hear her apologizing to someone around the corner before I have my door fully closed. Pulling it back open, I poke my head out, hoping it's not Vonnie and Lolita she's crossed paths with. Male voices respond to her, saying it's no problem and returning their own apologies.

The end of a massive couch comes around the corner, being manhandled by a barrel-chested guy with impossibly huge arms. That's got to be Vaughn's, not only because we're the only two people who live in this section of the hall, but that oversized leather monstrosity has his name all over it.

His bedding supply may be inadequate, but based on his plush mattress and his gym equipment, he buys quality stuff. This couch looks like it probably cost more than all my furniture combined.

The delivery guy sees me. "This coming to you?"

"No, it's going across the hall."

Vaughn opens his door. "I never had a delivery show up early before."

"They packed the truck light this morning, and you're our last stop. You're ready for it, right?"

"Oh, yeah. I'm not turning it away."

I step back and close my door to get out of the way.

A minute later, there's a knock. It's Vaughn. "Hey, it's pretty tight quarters out here We're trying to get this thing turned to bring it in. Can we open your door to make more space?"

"Yeah, sure. You know you bought a couch the size of a barge, right?"

"I like comfort."

I open my door wide and step away to watch from my living room. Vaughn helps the two delivery guys angle and shift the couch, moving it a few feet this way and that until one corner of it clears my doorway on its side. They keep going until it's partially in my apartment and partially in his, and then they set it down and Vaughn climbs over so he's also in my apartment. They all three maneuver the couch the rest of the way into his apartment.

Vaughn's door closes, so I close mine. All I want to do is run over there and get a better look at that giant, comfy couch, but I know they've still got to set it upright and push it into position. And then, knowing Vaughn, he'll probably offer them beers, and they'll hang around and watch some game on his new TV. Never mind that I haven't seen him all weekend, and I'm having withdrawal symptoms—tingly, needy sensations that were in no way diminished by watching his arms and back muscles flex as he shoved on that couch.

I would let him do dirty, dirty things to me on that couch. But he hasn't seemed to want for my attention all weekend. Wouldn't even come to the pool.

Voices drift back out into the hallway. He's thanking them. And they're leaving. Yes! Not that it means I get to hang out with him, but the chances are better now.

He knocks on my door and I yank it open way too excitedly. "Hi!"

"Hi. Did you friend leave?"

"Yeah. She nearly got crushed by your new couch on her way out."

"Oh, no. That would've been tragic."

"It was a close call."

"Well, I'm glad she wasn't crushed." He rests his forearms on either side of my doorframe and leans in, the same way he did at the door to my library that first night, except this time I'm standing so close there are only inches between us. "How about you? Are you in the mood to be crushed?"

"Completely."

He takes my hand and pulls me into the hall. I barely have time to reach back and grab my doorknob before it's out of reach. Our momentum is enough to slam my door, and he opens his just as quickly.

I barely get a glimpse of his couch before he's kissing me and walking me backwards toward it, his hands skating through my hair as we move, his tongue dueling with mine. He's not groping or shoving. His hands feel like they're casting a spell on me as they knead my scalp, and we're practically gliding together, perfectly in sync. It's a short distance, but the surprise of his eager touches and kiss literally took my breath away, forcing me to draw a deep inhale when we reach the couch and he ends the kiss.

With his hands still buried in my hair, he stares into my eyes and says, "I've been imagining you naked on this couch all day."

"It was probably really hot in the back of that delivery truck. I'd be in a terrible mood right now if I'd been naked on this couch all day."

He shakes his head gently, laughs softly. "You've got a smartass comeback for everything."

"I'm very witty."

"And so very pretty." His hands slip out of my hair and down to the bottom of my shirt. He slides it up my body, and I lift my arms to assist as he pulls it over my head. His fingers trace the lace edges of my bra at the swells of my breasts and it sends a shiver down my spine. He maintains eye contact as he unbuttons my shorts, slowly unzips them, and pushes them over my hips. They fall to the floor, and I step out of them.

He takes his time removing my bra, and finally lets his eyes leave mine when he drops to his knees to remove my panties, planting kisses over every inch of my skin as he reveals it. "Sit down," he says as he stands back up.

I drop to the edge of the cushion and he shakes his head. "Sit back."

Sliding back, I sit with my arms by my sides and let him look at me.

"Spread your legs."

He keeps his commands simple, but the effect his words and his eyes have on me is intense. Shallow breaths are all I can manage.

"Lie on your side, facing me."

His lucent gaze makes me feel more exposed with every new position. I despise being vulnerable, especially to men, but it's different with him. I want to be defenseless, to embrace the trembling exhilaration of not knowing what he'll do next, when he'll touch me or how.

"Roll onto your stomach." He steps closer but still doesn't touch me. I look up and over my shoulder. His eyes track down my body and back up again. "Get on your knees with your back to me."

Warm fingertips press between my shoulder blades. "Lean forward, rest your weight on the back cushion, and spread your legs."

Peak vulnerability engaged. The moment my head begins to turn to look at him, he says, "Let your head fall back so I can see your hair hang down your back."

His appreciative moan sets off a quiver that starts in my core and races downward, causing my pussy to clench. "Is this it?" I ask, teasingly. "You just want to look at me?"

"I already told you, I've been looking at you all day. But yeah, it's exactly what I want to do right now. Can I take your picture?"

My head lifts and swings to the side. "Do you promise you'll delete it?"

"While you watch, I promise. But I want to take more than one."

"So, you expect me to pose for you all afternoon?"

"Not all afternoon, beautiful. Just until I can't keep my hands off you for another second. Go ahead. Drive me crazy. You have more power over when this photoshoot ends than I do."

I arch my back to pop my ass out and drop my head so far back he can get my eyes in the shot. His groan is gruff and growly. "Yes. God, you're gorgeous."

It's easier with my back to him, but after a few minutes, I'm enjoying being his model, gaining enough confidence to spin around on my knees and lean my head back again, jutting my breasts toward him now. This earns more of his gravelly praise, which spurs me to sit all the way down.

Planting my feet with my knees bent, I spread them apart as far as I can for the fully unobstructed money shot. I shake my head, causing some of my hair to fall over my shoulders, obscuring my nipples but leaving all my curves visible, flashing him a bit-lip smile because I know that gets to him. He can mask a lot, but he responds to that with a devilish glimmer every time. Yeah, there it is.

I brush my hair back over my shoulders and pinch my nipples, keeping my upturned lip between my teeth. He snaps a pic and then tosses his phone on the far end of the couch and grabs my legs behind my knees, pulling me to the edge of the cushion where I originally sat. "Lie back. Let's officially christen this couch."

"Give me your phone," I say. "It's my turn to be the photographer."

"You got it." He retrieves his phone and hands it to me. I aim the camera at him, but instead of taking off his pants, he drops to his knees and presses my legs wider.

I have to hold the phone near my shoulder and angle it down to get a shot of him licking me. He cuts his eyes up at the phone and smiles. Then he extends his tongue and drags it slowly over my clit still staring right at the lens. He's not shy at all. I switch to video and watch him through the screen. Why is this so much hotter than watching him with my naked eyes? I lean back and reposition the phone so I can relax and still watch what he's doing.

He's always good at this, but he performs for the camera. My hands don't stay steady long enough to capture the full act. The phone falls to the cushion beside me when my breath hitches and my body starts to quake. Vaughn captures my clit between his lips. Behind my eyelids, I can see him doing it as clearly as if I were still watching him through his phone.

My back arches, and my ass lifts off the cushion as my quavering muscles begin to tense. I come on his face harder than any toy or any other tongue has ever elicited. Panting, he looks up at me and smiles.

"I think I wrecked your beard," I say through my own uneven breaths.

"And it's the only one I have."

We both laugh so loud that if he had neighbors, they'd think we were watching something hilarious on TV. Of course, a moment ago, they'd have thought we were watching porn. Having no neighbors is amazing.

Except someone does live below us. "Do you think our downstairs neighbors can hear what goes on in our apartments?"

"Some things, but this place is pretty well insulated."

"Some things like what?"

"Like if you dropped something heavy, they'd probably hear a thud on their ceiling." He rubs his hands up and down my outer thighs. "They can't hear you wrecking my beard."

"Not even through the air vents?"

"Oh, shit. I didn't think about the air vents."

My eyes fly open and he laughs again. "I don't think they can hear you through the air vents, Landry."

"Great. So, if I get murdered in my apartment, no one will hear me scream."

"If they heard anything through my air vents just now, I guarantee they did not think you were being murdered." He stands and peels his shirt off. I sit all the way up because I will never get tired of watching this man unveil his body.

Without warning, he whips his shirt behind my back and grabs the other end so he's holding it in opposite hands and using it like a strap to pull me forward. He bends down to kiss me. It's aggressive. His beard is still drenched, and I can taste myself on his tongue. "But," he says, pressing his cheek to mine. "I will always hear you if you scream, and I'll come running to save you. No matter what."

Tears sting the backs of my eyes, and they have nothing to do with the orgasm he just gave me, but I hope if he sees them, he thinks they do. I don't want to have to explain why the thought of him wanting to protect me could make me cry, especially not right now.

He sheds the rest of his clothes and we unabashedly break in his new couch. More sounds, more pictures, more video . . .

When I eventually convince him that I have to leave because I have laundry to do and need to call my mom so she won't send the cops to my door to check on me, he's the one who brings up deleting the pics. I watch him start deleting, but then I set my hand on his wrist. "Stop. If I want some of them, is that okay?"

"Do I get to keep them, too?" I hesitate, which is unfair, but I can't help it. "I can create a password protected folder for them. You can watch me do it."

Maybe I shouldn't trust him to do this, but if someone you've known the longest can hurt you the most, why can't it be true that someone new might be telling the truth when he says he'd do anything to keep you from getting hurt? "Pinky swear?"

I expect him to roll his eyes at that, but he smiles, extends his pinky, and nods reassuringly. I hook mine around it and he squeezes.

We agree which images and files to keep and which to delete. Our favorites are all the same. That probably means nothing, but right now, it kind of feels like everything.

I have never in my life had naked pics of myself on my phone, let alone videos. If I ever go missing and my phone is found before my body, some forensics IT person will find every one of them. But I'd probably have bigger things to worry about in that scenario, so fuck it.

These images are empowering in a way I wouldn't have imagined. Finding a folder full of personal porn wouldn't cause the police to close my case file. If it wouldn't matter then, why the hell should it matter now when no one is even looking for it? I'm safe. And I'm happy.

Vaughn

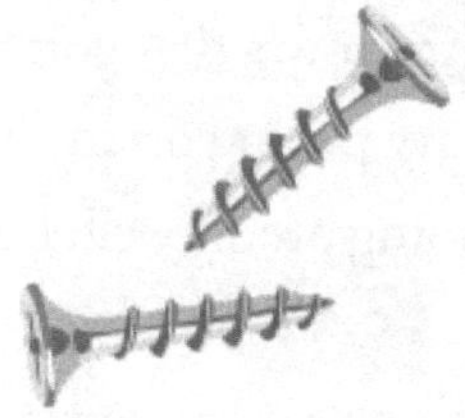

I PAUSE IN THE living room before I walk out to start a new week. That's a damn sexy couch. Best money I ever spent. And taking this job was the best fucking decision I ever made.

First on my agenda today is meeting with my preferred vendor to get the garage door back up and running.

Rex is already inspecting the problem when I get to the parking garage. This is why I use the guy. He shows up when he says he will and he's a straight shooter. "Hey, man. Got it fixed yet?"

He laughs and extends his hand. "I've got it diagnosed."

"The first guy who came out just wanted to sell us a whole new system."

"If you've got any money in the budget, I'd also like to give you a bid to replace it, but I can get it working in the meantime."

"They just did a full rehab on this place. I don't know why they didn't replace it then. All I can figure is they left a few things undone so the new manager could make some of her own decisions. Definitely get me the bid. I'm glad you can get it running for now, though. The tenants are wearing me out about it."

"New manager, huh? How's that going?"

A slideshow of Landry posing on my couch scrolls through my mind. "It's uh . . . it's going pretty well. I've definitely worked with worse."

"That's good. I don't have time to stop in and meet her today, but I'll get the bid worked up in the next day or two. Where do you want me to send it?"

"Email it to me." I hand him one of my cards. "I'll forward it to her."

"Cool. I'm not an approved vendor for your management company. Is there a link where I can find the requirements?"

"Give me your card and I'll have her email you about getting set up. Let me know when you send your stuff in. I'll make sure it gets expedited."

"If I fix this today, will I get paid or should I come back after I'm in the system as an approved vendor?"

"You'll get paid. You take care of me, I'll take care of you." We shake hands again, and I leave him to do his job. Damn, it feels good to work with people who don't make shit more complicated than it needs to be.

We don't have any open work orders right now. I've got Holden out walking the property to see if he comes across anything that needs attention. My guess is he's probably devoting most of his attention to the women at the pool.

Sure enough, that's exactly where I find him, slow-walking down the sidewalk, pretending he's not staring at a woman in an orange bikini through his sunglasses. I step up behind him, my footsteps muted by the music blaring from her wireless speaker shaped like a vintage radio. No bass, sounds terrible. "What'd she call you to fix?"

He jumps. "What? Who?"

"Go to the supply room on the eighth floor and organize it. It's a fucking mess. I don't even know what we've got in there."

"Seriously?"

"It's inside in an air-conditioned building. If you'd rather stay out in the heat, I guess you could pick up trash from fence line."

"I'll head up to the eighth floor."

"Good choice."

I stop by the office and toss Rex's card onto Landry's desk. "You'll see an invoice from this guy shortly. He's fixing the garage door. You can use the email address on his card to send him the link or whatever requirements he needs to get approved."

"You called a vendor who's not on our approved list?"

"I tried one from the list first. Didn't work out. This is my guy. He's good. He'll send over whatever we need."

"You can't just call whoever you want. That's why we have an approved list."

"If the list is full, kick off that first company I called because they suck. And you can replace them with Rex. Problem solved."

"You know we need his insurance before he works on any of our equipment. We need his paperwork on file. He has to sign things. I know you know this!"

"Are you having a rough Monday?"

"I am now."

I pick up Rex's card and walk it over to Carina's desk. "Can you email him and let him know what we need to get him approved?"

"Yes, but Landry's right. He's supposed to be approved before he does any work."

"I'll do it that way from now on."

Landry's exasperated sigh practically blows up the back of my shirt. I turn to face her again. "I promise. I'll follow the rules from here on out. But Rex is good. He's also going to send you a bid for a new door. The one we have is ancient. It should've been replaced as part of the rehab."

"That's true," Carina says.

"If it needs to be replaced, I'm going to have to get three bids." I've never seen Landry glare like she's doing right now. "Did you tell him that?"

"That three-bid requirement is a bunch of bureaucratic bull-shit."

"Well, apparently the Nouveau is a bureaucracy. Along with every other property in town. Three bids is standard procedure, Vaughn."

"But we'll approve his, right?"

"Not if his is the highest."

"He might not be lowest, but he won't be the highest. Let's make this easy. Get the first two and let me know what they are."

"And then you'll share those numbers with your buddy, so he can come in right between them?"

"He's not a buddy. He's the best vendor for the job."

Carina laughs. "Okay, to be fair, what's Vaughn's proposing is pretty standard practice, too."

I smile at Landry. "See? But you already knew that. Let's both stop pretending we don't know how shit works and just get it done. It'll make our lives easier."

"I'm not here to make your life easier. I'm here to do my job."

With my palms planted on her desk, I lean forward and look her in the eyes. "And as far as I can see, you're very good at your job. But I'm also good at mine. Can you please just call two other vendors and obtain bids? If Rex can't compete, then we'll use whoever we have to. But I want to give him a fair shot because he's good at his job, too, okay?"

"Why can't you be reasonable first? Why do you have to lead with all that bravado and piss me off to begin with?"

"I was being reasonable. I said here's the best option. Let's proceed. How is that unreasonable?"

"Please get out of the office before my head explodes."

She leaves her desk to refill her coffee. I turn to Carina and place my fists on either side of my head, flicking my fingers out to mime an explosion. Landry turns in time to see my splayed hands pulling away from my temples. "I saw that!"

I cross my forearms in front of my face defensively. "I'm going. I'm going." At least Carina thinks I'm funny this morning.

Vonnie whirls around the corner in a sea of blue and green fabric that falls behind her like a crashing wave. "Is Lolly on the loose again?" I ask.

"No, she's upstairs, safe and sound." She holds out her phone. "Can you help me? I installed one of those apps to get a ride to the auto parts store, but I don't know how to use it."

"Sure. But what's going on with your car?"

"My battery is dead. That sweet, young, curly-haired chiropractor from the fourth floor tried to jump-start it for me, but it's a goner."

"And you know how to replace a car battery?"

"How hard can it be? I assume you just unhook the old one and pop in the new one. Trust me, honey, I've replaced a million batteries in my lifetime." She winks.

"Car batteries?"

"Well, no."

"I'll show you how to use the ride app, but how about I give you a ride this time? And then I'll swap out the batteries for you."

"Are you sure you have time?"

"I'm positive."

"You are just as sweet as you are handsome."

"Can you mention that the next time you go in the office?"

"Uh-oh. What'd you do?"

"If you figure it out, tell me, and then we'll both know."

She cackles. I shouldn't have mentioned anything about the office, but having Vonnie on my side seems like a good idea, no matter the situation.

The auto parts place is less than two miles from The Nouveau, but she points out every store and restaurant along the way and tells me what it used to be. And what it was before that.

I make sure she gets the right battery. She takes an air freshener from a display at the register and adds it to her purchase. While her receipt is printing, she opens the air freshener and sets it on the counter. As we walk away, an employee yells, "Ma'am, you forgot your air freshener."

"No, I didn't," Vonnie calls back to him. "You leave that thing right where I put it. It stinks to high heaven in here. Y'all ought to be ashamed, having customers come in here and have to smell this place."

Truth be told, it smells like any other auto parts store, mostly like rubber and grease, though this one does have a strong note of transmission fluid, like someone's recently spilled a bottle. I doubt Vonnie's been in many of these places. I also don't think she'd accept that what she smells is normal, so I hold the door open for her and don't say a word. I get an earful about the stench on the drive back. She's going to write a letter to their corporate office to make them aware of the poor customer experience they're providing.

I grab a wrench from the toolbox in the bed of my truck, remove her old battery and install the new one. "Leave your receipt in my truck and I'll take the old battery back to the store for you tomorrow. There's a core charge they'll refund to you."

"Now, see," she says. "I wouldn't have even known to do that."

I wipe my hands on a rag. "I'll bring you the new receipt showing the amount they put back on your card."

"You are an absolute treasure."

"Again, if you could casually drop that into the conversation next time you're in the office, I'd appreciate it."

She promises to talk me up. "And I'll bake you some cookies, too."

"If you start baking for me, I might become your full-time driver."

"Careful what you offer, honey."

"You're all set to go, Vonnie."

"First, I need to run upstairs and spritz on a little more perfume, make sure I'm not walking around smelling like used motor oil."

The last thing she needs is more perfume, but I just smile and nod. "All right. Well, you be safe. I'm going to get back to work."

She serenades me as she crosses the parking garage to the elevators. Weirdly, that's starting to grow on me.

Landry

VAUGHN HAS AGITATED ME to no end all week. I swear, he's doing it on purpose. It doesn't help that everyone else can't stop singing his praises. Carina thinks he's so funny. Vonnie says he's just the sweetest hunk of manhood ever. Holden swears he's some kind of mechanical genius who can fix anything.

It's like he's paying people to say nice things about him. Every time they do, it annoys me more. I can't explain exactly what it is—it's just, everything about him.

The worst part is I can't even argue with any of their compliments. Yes, he's funny. And he can be sweet sometimes. And he does seem to fix everything with ease. Not to mention how easy he is to look at. There has to be something bad about him, though. No man is that good!

He's grumpy way too often and he's arrogant sometimes, too. But when his good traits show up, they make those things seem minor, and that feels like a trick, like a magician diverting the audience's eyes so they don't see the sleight of hand taking place.

I wish the big bad stuff would hurry up and surface so I can stop anticipating it. I get all antsy and edgy every time he comes in the office, and outside of work, even when I think I want to see him, as soon as an opportunity arises, I avoid it.

Last night, I was about to open my door to bring in my groceries when I heard him open his. He kept talking to the guy who'd dropped off my bags. And talking and talking. Finally, the guy said he had to get going. I peeked through the peep hole in my door, and Vaughn was staring right at me. He was still standing across the hall by his door, but it felt like he knew I was looking at him, like he was staring right through me.

Those groceries sat in the hall for fifteen minutes before I brought them in. My ice cream was half melted.

I check the time on my phone. Twenty minutes to go. This has been such a long Friday. It's supposed to rain all weekend, and the fact that I'm looking forward to being an antisocial hermit for two days should probably worry me, but I cannot wait to be all alone in my own space.

Carina invites me to go out with her and some of her friends, but I tell her I don't feel well. "Maybe next time," she says.

I didn't lie. I really don't feel great, but it's not illness.

The elevator stops on the second floor and I inwardly groan. All I wanted was an express ride to the top. I straighten my shoulders and prepare to smile and be nice to whichever tenant boards.

It's Vaughn. "Hey, beautiful."

"Hey."

"Why are you mad at me?"

"I'm not mad at you." The elevator doors close, and the car starts to move again. He reaches for the control panel and places the emergency stop button between his thumb and index finger. "Don't make me pull this."

"It'll call for help the moment you do it. The whole building will hear the alarm going off."

"Let them hear it." He grips the button tighter.

"Stop! Fine. We can talk, but do not trap us in this elevator. I'm claustrophobic, and I will freak the fuck out if you do that."

"Okay." He drops his hand. "Are you really claustrophobic?"

"Yes."

"Why didn't you ever tell me that?"

"I never expected you to try to trap me in an enclosed space."

"If my weight is on you, do you panic?"

"No, it's not that severe."

"Oh, good."

"Did you honestly think I'd been lying under you trying to hide a panic attack?"

"It's never seemed that way, but I was starting to think maybe I don't pay as careful attention to you as I thought I did."

You pay plenty of careful attention to me. But I'm not going to tell you that right now.

The doors open on our floor. "Your place or mine?" he asks.

"How about the roof?"

"Damn, we need neutral territory for this talk, huh?"

"It's going to storm all weekend. Might as well get some fresh air while we can."

"I assume you want to change clothes?"

"I'll meet you up there in a few."

"Don't stand me up. I know where you live."

I roll my eyes, but I can't help but smile a little as I'm doing it.

To my surprise, I beat him to the roof. I walk to the rail. Heavy gray clouds are gathering, darkening the sky and making it seem later than it is. Forecast is wrong again. So much for the storms holding off until tomorrow. The air already smells like rain. Like honeysuckle and fresh-cut grass, this is one of my favorite outside smells.

Vaughn doesn't leave me waiting long. His hair's wet. "You could've told me you were going to shower," I say. "I would've taken my time, too."

"I didn't expect you to get out here so fast." He sets his cooler down and unlocks the closet to get the chairs. He unfolds one and motions for me to take it. "You smell good."

"It's mosquito repellant."

He leans toward me and sniffs like he's not sure it's actually me that smells good. "Smells better than any bug spray I've ever used."

"It should for what it costs. It's organic, which probably means it doesn't work, but at least I'll smell good while I get eaten alive."

"You're funny even when you're mad."

"I already told you, I'm not mad."

"Yeah, you are. Why?"

"I don't know, okay?"

"Okay." He sits next to me and offers me a beer. He opens it before he hands it to me, and that pisses me off, which is dumb, but here we are. "Can we talk about it?"

"How are we supposed to talk about it if I don't even know what it is?"

"I think you do know."

"Of course, you do. You think you know everything."

"I don't really think that." He takes a swig from his bottle and wipes his mouth with the back of his hand. "But I know I can come across that way sometimes."

I'm stunned. I didn't expect him to humble himself right out of the gate like that. "Well, if you know, why don't you stop acting that way?"

"That I don't know. I guess it's just who I am."

"Nobody's perfect." The dripping sarcasm was unintentional. And unmistakable.

"Wow, so other than that, I'm perfect?"

"That's not what I said." My defenses soften. I don't want to fight with him, but I do want to stay mad. I want a barrier between us. And he's right, I do know why. "It was nice of you to fix Vonnie's car."

"All I did was put in a new battery."

"Whatever you did, you're her hero."

"I'm no hero." Lightning flashes in the distance. "We should go in."

"The storms weren't supposed to start until tomorrow."

"Well, the rain is about to start now."

Cold droplets hit my arms as if he conjured them. "Fine. You win."

We collapse the chairs and he shoves them back in the closet. I pick up the cooler, but he takes it away from me before I reach the door. "Your place or mine?" he asks again.

"Mine."

"I'm following you." He holds the door open for me to enter ahead of him.

"So you can watch my ass on the stairs?"

"Exactly."

As soon as the door shuts behind us, enclosing us in the short stretch of private stairwell, he drops the cooler. I spin around to see what happened, and he pins me to the wall. His kiss is hard and hungry. It's the first time we've kissed in days, and I match his intensity.

"I couldn't wait any longer to do that." He rests his forehead against mine. "Now, we can go inside and talk."

I wave my hand between us. "I'm following you."

Laughing, he picks up the cooler and leads me down the rest of the steps.

He sets the cooler on my kitchen counter, and I place my beer next to it. "I'm not really in the mood for beer tonight. If I open a bottle of wine, will you help me drink it?"

Contemplating the beer in his hand, he raises his eyebrows. "It's okay if you'd rather stick with beer."

"I'll drink wine with you." He pours our open beers down the sink while I open a bottle of wine. "Did you get a new coffee table?"

"It's not exactly new, but new to me, same as all my furniture."

"There's nothing wrong with secondhand furniture." He sits on my couch and puts his feet up on the edge of the coffee table. "It works just fine."

"You better take your shoes off it before I come over there and hit you in the head with this bottle." I laugh as I take glasses out of the cabinet.

"Tell the world I'd hope to see it with you," he says. "Interesting title."

I know without looking that he's picked up the book from my coffee table. I bring the bottle and glasses into the living room to pour. "It's poetry. I love Kristina Mahr. She writes a lot about the pain of broken relationships, but they read like they're about grief sometimes, too."

"I think people do grieve after a relationship ends." He takes the glass I offer. "Sometimes, anyway."

"You're probably right. I never thought about it like that. When I read her poems, I feel like they have all these layered meanings. They're mostly about a romantic relationship, but some of them seem like they could be about a bad relationship with parents, or anyone you love who didn't treat you the way they should have and let you down."

He nods. "I think there are a lot of similarities in that type of hurt."

"Yeah, I think so, too." I kick off my shoes and sit next to him, pull my legs up under me, and take a sip. We've been alone together in my apartment before; I shouldn't feel so much trepidation over drinking a glass of wine with him on my couch.

But the air between us is fraught with uncertainty tonight, a delicate sense of boundaries in jeopardy, defenses that could unravel at the slightest pull of a thread. There's no small talk that could shore up this mood, so I dive right into the deep. "Why'd you get divorced?"

"We were incompatible."

"Too vague."

"Okay." He takes a big gulp of his wine. "She was different from the women in my family. My mom and my aunts all catered to their husbands' every need, never did anything for themselves. Even most of the women I dated before her seemed to think being somebody's wife was the ultimate life goal. It impressed me, seeing a woman who was just entirely her own person. She was wild and impulsive, followed her own whims, thrived on taking risks. It actually fascinated the hell out of me. Until I realized I'd mistaken recklessness for independence."

"An independent person can still go through a reckless phase. I know I did."

"Some people are just reckless. By the time I recognized that about her, we were married, and she was completely dependent on me. Not an ounce of real independence about her."

"You felt responsible for her? Obligated?"

"Honestly? I felt trapped. Blamed her for a long time, but I let it happen. Saw what I wanted to see, ignored a whole lot of shit I should've paid attention to."

"What made you finally leave?"

He takes a long, slow pull from the rim of his glass, swallows like it's shards of glass going down. "I didn't. She left."

"For someone else?"

"They say there's a sucker born every minute. I was the only who let her stay, and he was the one who took her away. Left me with the bills she ran up, and a fuck-ton of regret."

"Do you still love her?"

"No. I don't think I ever did. I was infatuated for a while, but by the end, I was just... angry. I couldn't figure out how I'd let myself end up with someone like her. Then she did what I didn't have the courage to do. It was so easy. All I ever had to do was leave, but I was too weak to end it."

"I think maybe you were too strong to end it. Strong-willed. Sometimes that's admirable. Other times, it's sheer goddamn stubbornness. Some people have to live it to learn it."

"Quit acting like you know me." His smile quirks. "What finally gave you the courage to leave your ex?"

I shrink back at the question. "I don't know that anybody could call my exit courageous. He went on a weekend fishing trip with his brother, and I packed up all my clothes and disappeared. Left a note on the counter, put the whole experience in my rearview mirror and drove as fast I could to the dorm room I'd already secured, moved in, and tried to pretend I was just like everybody else."

"Why'd you do it that way?"

"Path of least resistance." I shrug. "He hated that I went to community college thirty minutes away. He'd have never moved with me so I could finish school. We were done, anyway. I knew how mad he was going to be that I'd made all the decisions and arrangements behind his back, but I was going, no matter what. So, I figured why bother with the argument, you know? A clean break was best."

"Was it an argument you didn't want to bother with or a temper you didn't want to set off? Were you afraid of him?"

Fuck. What did I say? I hate being caught off guard, but Vaughn has a knack for zeroing in on exactly what I don't want to reveal.

He sees right through me. "Not when other people were around. He was Prince Charming for an audience. But he'd have never had that conversation in front of witnesses. I'd been *his* since I was sixteen. If I was leaving him, he would've wanted to talk privately."

"Only insecure pieces of shit need to put their hands on a woman like that. You probably know that, but it bears saying, anyway."

"Yeah, well, insecure piece of shit about sums him up. Nobody knew." I try to blink back tears, but it's no use. A stream rolls down my cheeks. "So many people back home called me a selfish bitch for taking off like that. They sent me messages, posted their opinions all over social media. I'd broken his heart. Destroyed his whole life. I didn't even try to explain, just cut ties and never looked back, let them believe whatever they wanted about me."

"There were people who knew." He pulls me close and squeezes tight. I rest my head on his shoulder. "There are always people who know. Probably some of the same ones who called you a selfish bitch for leaving him. Small minds living small lives. I can't believe you got yourself out of that situation all alone."

"I didn't do it alone. An advisor at school referred me to resources I didn't even know existed." I sniffle against his shirt. "I was almost twenty-one-years-old, and complete strangers had to help me figure out how to get a divorce. And how to survive while doing it."

"You were too damn young to get married in the first place. How were you supposed to know how to get a divorce?" He pulls away, and I force myself to meet his gaze. "Those miserable fucks back in your hometown who talked shit about you? Most of them probably envy the hell out of you now. And they might never tell you, but I guarantee you're somebody's inspiration. Every time bad thoughts about what you went through back then creep in, you think about that instead."

I hear Jenna's voice, telling me she's proud of me. "Thanks."

Thunder crashes and rain slaps against the windows. The storm definitely blew in early.

We drink wine and listen to Mother Nature rage. For a long time, no words pass between us, but it's a comfortable silence. Drowsiness rolls over me like a warm blanket. The combination of the storm and the wine will have me sleeping like a baby in no time if I give in to it, but I don't want to sleep yet. "Any chance you want to carry me to bed?"

He smiles. "A pretty strong chance."

His kisses are soft when we're naked together between my sheets. His touch is soft, too. "Don't do this," I say. "Don't treat me like I'm breakable because of my past."

"I want to be gentle with you tonight. Let me."

I let him for as long as I can, but I need to know he doesn't see me as weak now. I need him to confirm with actions, not words. "If you really don't see me as fragile, prove it."

"Do you honestly think I'd lie to you about that?"

"I don't know. Maybe. Show me I'm wrong."

"Has anybody ever mentioned you might be a brat?"

"Maybe you should spank me then." I tug on his beard to bring him in for a kiss, but I pull harder than I mean to. He arches his eyebrows as if to send a warning. So I do it again.

Vaughn

"Quit looking at porn while you're on the clock." Holden laughs like it was totally okay for him to float that jab as he comes around the corner, sneaking up on me like a goddamn leopard in socks.

I clutch my phone and tell myself all the reasons it would be a bad idea to kick his skinny little ass right now. "You proud of that joke?"

"Sorry. Feeling myself a little this morning. I got good feedback on some new scenes last night."

"Congratulations. That trash along the fence line isn't going to pick itself up."

"Okay, I'm on it. It's from all those little rich kids that walk past here on their way home from school. They just toss their empty wrappers and water bottles like the whole world is their trash can."

"If they all did it, picking up their trash would be your full-time job. Be glad it's only a few of them."

He takes a trash bag from the box on the shelf behind him and heads out. A man can't even look at his phone in peace in a damn supply closet. It's not porn, but it is Landry posing like a porn star on my couch. It's hard to believe that was almost two months ago. So much has changed since then. I know her now, really know her, and she doesn't seem too young anymore. She knows a frightening amount about me, too, and she hasn't told me to get lost yet. God, she's beautiful. I close the image and slip my phone into my pocket.

"Hey, there you are!"

Jesus, how many people are going to sneak up on me in this closet? Looking at her in person is even better than seeing her on my phone. I reach for her hand, but she whisks it away too fast. "Nice try, but you're not pulling me into this closet right now. Your buddy Rex is here with his guys to install the new garage door. He asked if you were around. I think he wants you to go out to the parking garage with him."

"You got lucky this time."

"He knows about us, doesn't he?"

"Rex? Hell, no."

"Are you sure? He looks at me like he knows."

"I haven't told him anything. I haven't told anyone anything. As far as I know, the only person who knows is your friend, Jenna. And I'm not the one who told her either."

She pauses for a beat too long. I knew it.

"How'd you know I told Jenna?"

"I could tell by the way she looked at me when I met her."

"Wrong. I just told her last week on the phone. She thinks she encouraged me to flirt with you and that's how it all started."

"She encouraged you to flirt with me?"

"Yeah, because she could tell you were into me."

"Jenna's got good instincts." I reach for her again, but she's steps away. "Fine, if you need me, I'll be in the parking garage, feeling rejected."

She laughs as we head in opposite directions, but I'm only halfway out the side door when she shrieks. I run around the corner to check on her and find her with her back pressed firmly against the wall. "I'm fine. It's just Lolita," she says, holding still as a statue. Her eyes are fixed on the carpet, where the red and orange snake stands out clearly against the gray and white houndstooth pattern.

"Come here, Lolly." I pick her up and call out for Vonnie. No answer. "Where is she?"

Landry shrugs. I head for the office, and she follows. Vonnie isn't in there, but Autry McDaniel is, and he goes ballistic when he sees the snake in my hands. "Call animal control! That snake is loose more often than it's in her apartment these days."

"I don't think we really want to do that, Autry."

Vonnie makes her appearance, cloaked in a mass of bright orange flowing fabric. I pass Lolita over, and the snake immediately wraps around her owner, looking like a coordinating belt for the dress. Vonnie's hair is held back by a thick black headband with a giant sequined sunflower on it. Such a big personality for such a little woman. And a big voice, which she's directing at Autry as I make my exit, leaving Landry to deal with the original two and our resident wandering snake.

Rex and his crew are all set in the parking garage, but I hang out and shoot the shit with him for a bit while they get started. He doesn't show me any signs he thinks I've got something going on with Landry. I wonder if he was flirting with her in the office. He wouldn't be the first vendor to do it. They all flirt with her. Even the FedEx guy hits on her.

If I bring it up, she laughs and points out every woman she thinks hits on me, including the woman in 501, who went topless at the pool over the weekend and nearly caused a damn riot. She kept insisting she didn't have to cover up because it's not illegal in Texas for a woman to be topless in public as long as she isn't causing a disturbance. I personally don't see why it should've mattered to anyone, but no less than half a dozen residents called to complain. A disturbance was undeniably caused.

Now 501 is in a feud with some of her neighbors. And she probably hates Landry because I made her deliver the news that we apparently have Puritans on the premises who can't handle themselves around bare tits. I'm sure she said it more professionally, which is why she was the better messenger. I don't have the patience for half the shit grown-ass people freak out over.

"Vaughn! Can I talk to you for a moment?"

I slow my steps and let Autry catch up. "Your ceiling's not leaking again, is it?"

"No, no leaks to report. But something needs to be done about that snake."

"Autry, that snake is Vonnie's companion."

"Well, what about the rest of us who might like a companion?"

"You've lost me."

"I might like to get a small dog."

"Okay. I'm pretty sure you just have to let the office know, and pay a pet deposit."

"I understand the requirements per my lease. But I'd like to be able to walk my little dog without worrying about it being eaten right off the end of its leash."

"Lolita is a corn snake, not a python. You wouldn't need to worry about her eating your dog."

"You can't guarantee it wouldn't happen."

"I am extremely confident it would not." I stop walking. "Do you know how long Vonnie has had Lolita?"

"Oh, she's always had one of those orange snakes. This is at least her third one. I guess she got her about five years ago."

"So, you know this snake could be around for a long while still. Do you really want to fight with Vonnie about her for the next ten years?"

"I don't want to fight with that woman about anything. I just want her to keep her snake in her apartment."

"Autry, get a dog. Enjoy it. It'll be fine." I start walking again, but he doesn't come along.

"And what if it isn't?"

He's going to keep me out here all damn day. "Are you worrying about your future dog in general now?"

"Anything could happen, you know? Companions aren't inde-structible." He turns and walks in the opposite direction, and I understand too late that this whole conversation has been about something else entirely. He's scared of loving something and losing it. I definitely could've handled that better. *Shit.*

I hide out in the supply room on the eighth floor for the rest of the afternoon. Holden did a good job organizing it, but I've already made a mess of it again. I restack shelves and pick up screws and washers from the floor.

A red-tailed hawk lands on the window ledge. I stare at him for a minute, but he doesn't fly away. Moving with small, even steps, I get closer. He doesn't budge. I'm able to walk all the way to the window without him flying away. "Why are you watching me?"

I laugh, realizing he's probably thinking the same thing. My fingertips touch the glass. He tilts his head and looks up at my hand, but he doesn't take off. "What are you doing hanging out up here? Are you hiding like me?"

"Hey, what are you doing in here?" Landry's voice puts an instant smile on my face.

"Just talking to this hawk." He lifts off before she steps into the room.

"A hawk?"

"Yes, Landry. There was a hawk outside the window. I'm not losing my mind."

"Cool. What were y'all talking about?"

"Close the door and come over here and I'll tell you."

She closes the door and walks to the window. "What did the hawk have to say?"

"He said a beautiful princess was going to show up soon in need of a magic carpet ride."

"If your beard is the magic carpet, I'm not riding it in here."

"Why not? We're all alone." I wrap my arms around her and pull her body to mine.

"Unless the hawk comes back."

"He won't mind. It was his idea."

She laughs into my chest. "I'm not getting on this floor in any way. It's filthy."

"It's just a little dust." I stretch my arm out and pull a desk chair from the corner. The casters spin, and I nearly lose control of it. "Here. You sit. I'll kneel."

"Wow. You're really afraid to disobey that hawk."

"He was pretty insistent that it needed to happen." She doesn't argue when I reach for her zipper. I fold her pants and lay them over the back of the chair, put her panties in my pocket. "Sit. Drape your legs over the arm rests."

"That's so indecent."

"I know."

She lowers her ass to the chair, leans back, and hooks her knees over the padded arms. The sight of her pretty pussy on display for me has me on knees with my next breath. This chair might be coming home with me.

I pull on the seat to bring her closer. The first taste makes me salivate. I inhale her scent and press the tip of my tongue inside her. She moans, and my cock twitches. Too bad this chair's not sturdy enough to fuck in. My tongue flattens against her delicate skin, and she weaves her fingers into my hair. The door cracks—"Out!" I yell.

It shuts as abruptly as it opened. Landry bolts upright. "Who was it?"

"Holden."

"Oh, shit. This is bad, Vaughn."

"It's okay. He couldn't have seen anything other than your bare leg, if that much. The back of the chair is too wide for him to have seen you, not even your hair.

"Are you sure?"

"Yes. I don't even think he saw enough to know what was happening." *But if he saw those white pants hanging there, he's probably got a hell of a clue about what and who. Fuuuuck me. Maybe he didn't notice what she was wearing today.* "He's probably scared shitless right now. I doubt he'll ever mention it, but if he does, I'll tell him it's none of his damn business, which is true."

"He's going to figure it out, Vaughn. People are starting to know. I can feel it."

"You're worried about people knowing. That's what you feel. Nobody knows anything."

"I'm scared to leave this room."

"He probably broke a land speed record running for the stairs." That gets a smile out of her. "Do you want to spend this weekend at the beach?"

"The whole weekend?"

"The whole weekend. Just you and me. No sneaking around. No looking over our shoulders."

"That sounds so good."

"It will be better than good. It'll be perfect."

I peek out to be sure the hallway's empty. We walk to her door, and I crowd her as she inserts her key in the lock. "What do you think you're doing?" she asks.

"I'm going inside with you. If that hawk comes back and asks if I followed through, I don't want to have to lie."

She gives me a full laugh this time. I wrap an arm around her waist and pull her away from the door. "On second thought, let's go to the roof."

"Why the roof?"

"Because you like the thrill of knowing you could get caught as much as I do, but no one will really catch us up there."

"Someone from another building could see us."

"I'll set a chair inside the closet. We'll leave the door open to shield us. AC units will block the view from the other side."

"It's hot up there."

"You can take off all your clothes."

The elevator dings and I freeze, listening to see if someone is coming or going. Sometimes I forget other people live on this floor, too. I'm getting too comfortable. Careless. Vonnie is talking softly to Lolita as she exits the elevator. "We don't have to stay in our apartment. That man can kiss both our asses. You and me like to roam, don't we, Lolly Girl?"

I slap my access card against the reader and pull the door open, ushering Landry into the roof stairwell with me. Keeping the doorknob turned, I gently push the door closed and let the knob unwind slowly until the lock engages. It echoes, but hopefully, that was only on our side.

"Let's go get dirty on the roof."

Landry

Vaughn props the closet door open to block the view from the left. He sets up one of his folding chairs at the threshold. "Take off your pants and have a seat." His tone carries a hint of challenge, and his eyes hold a questioning look. He's not sure I'll actually do it. "If you want to take off more, that's fine, too."

I'm definitely not taking off more. "Are you really going to kneel on the ground out here?"

"I'm wearing jeans, princess. They're washable."

"You call me princess a lot, but I actually prefer queen."

"I bet you do. Take off your pants and I'll treat you like one."

There's no doubt he will, but we could do this inside. He's not wrong that I like the possibility of getting caught; it's exciting, but this is so out in the open it feels more like a place to intentionally put on a show instead of hiding and hoping no one sees.

His fingers touch my chin, and he turn my face to his. "Sit down. See how enclosed it feels. If you still feel too exposed, we'll go back inside. Fair enough?"

Huh. Weird. It really does feel much more secluded now that I'm sitting. I hop back up to standing. He smiles. "Ready to surrender your pants, my lady?"

I step out of my shoes and surrender. My panties are still in his pocket, so I'm bare from the waist down. Standing brings back the anxious doubt about being out here like this. He carefully drapes my pants over the back of the chair, but when I attempt to sit, he catches me by the forearms and pulls me back up for a kiss.

While his tongue tangos with mine, he starts to inch my shirt up. "I'm not getting naked on the roof," I say, adamantly.

"What if I beg?"

"You don't beg."

"What if I bribe you?"

"I can't be bribed."

"What if I just admit how badly I want to see you naked on this roof right now?"

"Don't do that thing with your eyes. That's manipulation."

"If my eyes are doing anything, they're acting on their own. Come on, it's not even illegal for a woman to be topless in public."

That makes me laugh. "Unless it causes a disturbance."

"It's just you and me. And I promise not to be disturbed. Besides, your state of undress right now is actually illegal. You're already breaking the law. Taking off the rest of your clothes is minor by comparison."

"And I thought my reckless days were over." I pull my shirt over my head.

"A reckless moment now and then never hurt anybody."

"Pretty sure that's not true. Whole lives get changed by one reckless decision all the time."

He kisses me again. "This reckless moment won't hurt you. I promise."

I let him remove my bra with no resistance. Sitting back down in the chair, I spread my legs and place them over the arms without him having to ask.

"Damn, you are a most benevolent queen."

"Make sure the history books get it right."

"Not everything has to be documented. Sometimes, it's enough that the ones who were there when it happened know how it went down." With that, he winks. And goes down.

The breeze is warm and so is his mouth. I've been with other guys who had good oral skills, but Vaughn's are my favorite by far. I never have to shift or encourage him to do more or less of anything. He just knows.

I've never been naked, or even topless, in a public space like this before. It's strange and freeing, but I can't stop opening my eyes to glance around.

He stops and looks up at me. "Relax. Close your eyes. Don't even think about where you are."

I close my eyes, but I don't want to stop thinking about where I am. He sucks my clit, and my legs try to close, despite hanging over the sides of the chair. His hands are firm at the base of my inner thighs, keeping me open for him. My back arches and the tremors overtake me. Without his hands dropping to grasp the legs of the chair, I'm sure it would've tipped over, but with his legs free from the strength of his hands, they draw toward one another, trapping his face while he licks me through the aftershocks.

Fuck, that was amazing. I meant to say those words out loud, but they got derailed by a final shudder. I'll tell him later.

He stands and unbuttons his jeans. I'm not sure if what he has in mind is going to work. This chair seems too low for me to suck his dick without tilting my head back at a ninety-degree angle. I aim to please, but I'm not aiming for whiplash.

With his boots removed and set aside, he takes off his pants and folds them. And then he drops them to the ground between my legs. "Get on your knees, your majesty."

"So noble."

"Work quick and you won't have to be down there long."

I drop to my denim kneeling pad, take his cock in my hand and circle the crown with my tongue, licking away the precum that's leaked while he pleasured me, palpating the thick vein on the underside with my thumb, working my way up until my hand meets my mouth. His fingers weave into my hair, pulling me closer. Taking as much of his girth as I can into my mouth, I hollow my cheeks, begin to bob my head and my hand, twisting both in opposite directions, his knees soften for a moment before he locks them.

Helicopter blades thump overhead, but Vaughn won't let me pull off. His hands fist in my hair, and he thrusts his dick deeper. I choke a little, and my eyes water, but I keep going.

"Yeah, that's my girl. Keep taking it just like that. Fuck, you're incredible. Show me those eyes."

He doesn't stop me from pulling off enough to look up at him. His dick surges in my mouth the moment we make eye contact. When I look away and go back to the corkscrew technique I had going earlier, his body tenses. His thighs shake, and I brace myself for his orgasm to spill over my tongue. I feel victorious when it happens. That was quick work indeed.

The combination of having my legs spread over the arms of the chair and then bent underneath me with only a few layers of his jeans between my knees and the ground have left them trembling. He helps me to my feet and I lose my balance. His embrace steadies me. As soon as I'm sure on my feet, I'm ready to put my pants back on.

"Can I have my panties back?"

"What's the magic word?"

"I am twenty-six-years-old. I don't use magic words."

"What do you mean you're twenty-six? How?"

"That's what normally happens after someone has been twenty-five for a while. A year, to be specific." I laugh and hold out my hand for my panties. "My underwear? Please."

"Your birthday came and went and you didn't say anything?"

"It's just another day. It's not a big deal."

"I would've helped you celebrate it, Landry. Did anyone?"

"Yeah. My parents and my grandma called and sent cards. The usual."

"But you spent it alone? Doing nothing?"

"Well, I intended to hang wallpaper, but the delivery got delayed."

"When was your birthday?"

"Two weeks ago."

"Is the wallpaper here now?"

"Yes, but I haven't felt like hanging it since it got here. I sure don't feel like doing it tonight."

"Neither do I, but it'll get done this weekend."

"Thanks. Now, can I have my panties?" He pulls them from his pocket, and I dress as fast as I can. "I thought we were going to the beach this weekend."

"We are. I'll hire someone to hang your wallpaper."

"You don't have to do that."

"Consider it your birthday present."

Gifts make me uncomfortable, and that seems like a big one, but it's thoughtful. And I know he'll be upset if I refuse it. "Thank you."

He beams. I may not love receiving gifts, but I think he likes giving them. "Let's grab showers, and I'll cook you dinner," he says as he zips up his jeans. For the love of sweet tea, him offering to cook me dinner while his hand is on his zipper is ridiculously sexy. "On second thought, I'll take you to dinner. I haven't been to the grocery store in a while."

"I keep telling you there's an easy way around that."

We step through the first door into the hot stairwell. I definitely need a shower. "That helicopter scared the shit out of me."

"I know." He laughs. "It was Life Flight. They weren't worried about us."

"All I could think was I didn't want to be responsible for a helicopter crash."

Vaughn holds the second door open for me. "Listen, your oral skills are pretty damn good, but you're not about to cause helicopters to fall out of the sky."

I shove his shoulder as I walk past. "Shut up. Jerk. You know what I meant."

He wraps me up in the hallway before we turn toward our own doors. "And you know I was just teasing." He kisses my forehead. "You could totally suck a helicopter out of the sky."

"You better shower fast. I'm ordering the most expensive thing on the menu at dinner."

"You can have whatever you want." He releases the embrace, but stands in the middle of the hallway, watching me until I walk into my apartment and close the door behind me.

What the hell were we thinking, being all clingy in the hallway like that? And now we're going to dinner together? We're just asking to get busted. We definitely need to get away this weekend and get all this unguarded lovey-dovey stuff out of our system, recalibrate, and come back with our defense mechanisms reset.

While we're at the beach, we can pretend we're a regular couple. But when the weekend is over, it's back to reality. All we have to do is get through the rest of this week.

Vaughn

I WAIT UNTIL I hear Landry open her door to head across the hall. It took me all of fifteen minutes to shower and change. She needed over half an hour.

She smiles when I step out to meet her. Her hair is in a messy bun, and she's not wearing any makeup. She's gorgeous all dolled up, but I like seeing her natural like this. "What happened?" She points to the uniform shirt in my hand.

"It's got oil stains that won't come out." I shake it loose so she can see for herself.

"Did you wear it while you changed the oil in your truck?"

"It's a work shirt. I was working on my truck."

"Did you intentionally spill oil on it?"

"I think the word spill implies an accident. I don't know that you can intentionally spill something. At that point, you're pouring, not spilling."

"And you're deflecting, not answering."

"No answer is going to save this shirt." I drop it down the trash chute as we walk past. "I'm down to three, by the way."

"I'll order you more tomorrow. Blue, right?"

"Yes. And not light blue."

"Come to the office and look at the book. You can pick the color. Does Holden need new shirts already, too?"

"No, his are fine."

A tenant opens his door and steps into the hallway. Landry and I both immediately sidestep put more distance between us. We say hi to the tenant, and the three of us walk on together. When we walk past the elevator, it's apparent we're all headed for the stairs to the parking garage. I am so damn sick of having to worry about who sees what around here.

Jesus, does this guy have to match us step for step?

He spurs off with a wave when we reach the garage, not bothering to watch which way we go. Why would he be interested in what we're doing? He doesn't know if we're fraternizing after hours, and he wouldn't care if he did.

The wallpaper hangers are a mother-daughter duo that Wick recommended. They show up while Landry's still shoving last-minute choices into her bag for the beach. She takes a break from packing to give the two women such detailed instructions I'm surprised the mom doesn't kick her out of her own apartment. The woman assures Landry she'll send her pictures when it's all done. I finally convince her to leave. "They know what they're doing. They've got this.

She stares at my duffle bag. "It's obvious we're both headed out of town. We can't walk out together."

"You want to know who cares what we do together? The owners. Do you think Carina cares? I don't think so. The tenants? Why they fuck would they? Nobody else cares. And the owners aren't here. Let's go to Galveston and not worry about them or anybody else."

Her smile tells me everything I need to know. She wants to let go and stop worrying. I know she won't relax until we're on the island, which is all the more reason to hurry up and get there.

I've spent the weekend in Wick's beach house before, but not alone. It's strange to put the key in the lock and open the door like I own the place.

When we walk inside, Landry gasps. "Wow. This is so nice."

"He was dating an interior designer when he bought it. This is all her handiwork." She looks around like she's no longer sure about staying here. "Don't worry. I know how to disable all the cameras."

"Don't joke about cameras." She laughs and steps out of her shoes. I love watching her anxiousness slip away.

We tick off all the boxes on the first-night-at-the-coast checklist: late dinner, walk on the beach, shower together, fuck like we don't even know the meaning of the word stress, sleep like babies. When I wake up in the morning, I reach for her under the covers, the same way I did the first time we shared a bed. She wiggles under my touch and smiles without opening her eyes.

"Good morning," I whisper.

"Hi." Her eyes flutter open. "How long have you been awake?"

"Since about two seconds before I touched you."

"Don't stop touching me, but stop looking at me."

"Why would I want to do that?"

"My hair was still wet when we went to bed. I probably look like Medusa."

"That would be awful for you, seeing as how you're afraid of snakes."

"True. But you're not."

"No, I'm not." I kiss her shoulder. "Guess what?"

"What?"

"They have extra sheets here."

"Are we about to make a mess?"

"Oh, yeah."

Breakfast is always bigger at the beach. When the waitress brought out my plate with the giant omelet sitting on a bed of home fries, it looked like enough food for three people. But I finish it all with no regrets. "I apparently worked up an appetite this morning."

Landry takes the last bite of her pancakes. "Same. Now I'm ready to lie in the sun like a beached whale for a few hours."

"Are you sure you don't want to go for a run?"

"If you run after eating all that, you're going to puke on the beach."

"I'm not running this morning. But I'm not one for lying in the sun either. Wick's got lacrosse bats. We could toss the ball back and forth for a while. If you've never done it, I could teach you."

"That sounds like it requires running, or at least jogging after the ball, so, no."

"Boogie board?"

"Chair."

"There should be a service that lets you adopt a dog for the weekend when you come to the beach."

"And return it to the shelter on your way home? That's so mean."

"I miss having a dog."

"Get one."

"I like big dogs, and it wouldn't be fair to have a big dog in an apartment."

"Plus, your lease has a forty-pound weight limit for pets."

"Eh, I'm sleeping with the manager. I'm not worried about that."

She wads up the paper from her straw and flicks it at me. I bat it away with my hand, and it skids off the edge of the table as the waitress sets our ticket down. She gives us both the stink eye. This restaurant is full of hyped-up kids, throwing shit around. The last thing she needs is adults adding to the mess. I tip her well, and pick up the straw wrapper before we leave.

I lie next to Landry in a beach chair until I think my food has settled enough to run. It doesn't really matter because I can't be still for another minute. I'm running, regardless. Besides, she's reading a book, and every time I talk to her, she sighs before she answers me. I swap my flip-flops for running shoes.

The sand is hard-packed at the water's edge and it feels good under my feet. This is what I needed. I have to weave around dogs and kids, but it's still good.

My run is interrupted by a couple boys hovering over a Portuguese man o'war, their voices being carried on the breeze as they exchange dares about touching it. They look to be about eight, maybe nine, and they're obviously clueless about the creature. "Don't ever touch one of those," I say, slowing as I approach them.

"It's just a dead jellyfish," one of them declares like he's a miniature marine biologist and I'm clearly an idiot.

I tell them the real name, which they think is pretty cool. "Its tentacles are still venomous, even when they're washed up on the sand like this. And their sting is super painful."

"That thing can still sting me?"

"Yes. That's why you never want to touch one of these guys, okay?"

"Okay. Thanks."

I'm not even out of earshot when one dares the other to poke it with a stick. I laugh as I pick up the pace.

Landry's walking toward the water when I jog back. I watch her wade in to cool off. A wildly tossed football hits her in the back, and I look around defensively to see whose ass I need to kick. A teenage girl runs toward the waves and apologizes. Landry laughs, scoops the ball from the top of the water and throws it back, pausing first to line her fingers up on the laces. Perfect spiral.

I toe my shoes and socks off and wade in behind her. "Where'd you learn to throw like that?"

"You mean like a girl?" she shouts back.

The sun glints off the water all around her. "You threw that ball like a pro."

"Women can be pros now. There's literally a professional women's tackle football league."

I throw my arms up in surrender. "I know. I just didn't know you played for them."

She laughs and splashes water in my direction. "Well, don't underestimate me again."

"I wouldn't dream of underestimating you." I lift her up and spin her around. She wraps her arms around my neck. "Your shoulders are getting a little pink."

"I used sunscreen," she says. "But they'll be covered in freckles by the end of the weekend. They'll pop up across my nose, too."

"Freckles are sexy."

"It's a good thing you think so."

Water laps at the backs of my knees while I delve into her salty kiss. The football goes off course again, hitting the side of my head this time, disrupting our perfect warm kiss. "She's not going pro anytime soon," I joke.

Landry scrunches up her nose, smiles and shakes her head "No, probably not."

I send the ball sailing back to its unskilled player, and we leave the water for safer ground. I'm tired enough now to lie still in my chair while she reads some more. The soundtrack of waves and seagulls seems more relaxing than I usually find it.

My eyes blink open against bright sunlight. "I fell asleep?"

"You took a little nap. You must've needed it." She closes her book. "We probably don't need any more sun today, though. I know I don't, anyway."

"Let's go get something to eat."

"How can you possibly be hungry again already?"

"How can you not be hungry? Breakfast was hours ago."

We're seated on the patio of a seafood place overlooking the beach when she gets the text with pics of her new wallpaper. "It looks so good!" She turns her phone to show me.

"Happy Birthday."

"Thanks. She said she dropped my extra key back off at the office. Carina is still working. I feel guilty being at the beach while she's working on a Saturday."

"Hire a second leasing agent."

"That's my plan, but it's not easy when she takes on so much work. To the owners, it probably looks like we don't need anyone else, but she shouldn't be working every Saturday. It's not fair."

"I agree. But you deserve to be relaxing at the beach."

"It's pretty great not having to look over our shoulders or sneak around."

"Yeah, but I kind of like sneaking around with you."

"Okay, that is fun. Except when we get caught."

"That's only happened once." I watch her take a sip from her water glass as the breeze blows through her hair. She looks happy—the way she should always look. "Do you want to go to The Strand?"

"What is that?" she asks.

"Shopping. Bars. It's near the cruise terminal. The tall ship Elisa is docked there if you want to check that out."

"Do you come down here a lot?"

"I practically grew up on this island."

"Really? That's wild to me. I was in high school the first time I saw the beach, and I didn't see it again until I moved to Houston."

"No shit? That's wild to me. I can't imagine growing up so far from the coast." I finish off my tea. "Let's go be tourists."

There's a cruise ship leaving port. Landry can't take her eyes off it as we drive past. "Those ships are so huge. Have you ever been on a cruise?"

"Nope. Never going on one either. Every time you turn around, there's a story about how all the passengers caught some terrible virus or the ship lost power and everybody had to sleep on the decks."

"Yeah, but that's probably only a small percentage of them. You always hear about the bad stuff. It's not newsworthy to show a bunch of healthy happy people all safely enjoying their cruise."

"I'll never know."

The Strand is packed, but I get lucky and turn just as a car is leaving a great parking spot. I stop and give them room to get out.

"Oh, you have parking karma," she says. "I was not blessed with that. But I can't parallel park, anyway, so I'd have to leave this spot for someone else to get lucky."

"You can't parallel park? What do you do, just keep driving around until somebody finally leaves a spot you can pull straight into?"

"Yep. That's exactly what I do."

"That's uncalled for."

"Works for me."

"How are you so independent and competent, but you can't parallel park?"

"It's not a requirement for a successful life, I promise."

I claim the open parking space using the life skill she doesn't find necessary. We step out of the truck, and I walk around to take her hand. I've never been able to openly hold her hand. People take simple things like hand holding for granted, but on a day-to-day basis, I can't reach for hers. I like the way it feels in mine. "I could teach you how to parallel park."

"Thanks, but I have zero interest in learning how to master that."

"How can you not want to learn something?"

"Oh, there are plenty of things I want to learn. How to speak Spanish, do a fishbone braid, calligraphy, make the perfect peanut butter frosting, ice skate . . ."

"Aside from the second language, none of that shit's useful."

"I'd make use of it."

She pulls me into a store full of stuff nobody needs: candles in white ceramic conch shells, mermaid Christmas ornaments, big-ass silver starfish—she'll probably buy one of those for her bookshelves. Speaking of books, they apparently sell those in here, too. And, of course, she's got her hands on one. "Look!" She shouts like I'm not standing right next to her. "A recipe for peanut butter frosting. I just mentioned that and here it is. It's a sign. I'm buying this cookbook."

"You believe in signs?"

"I believe in this one."

I'd get her a whole case of those cookbooks to see her face light up like that. "Give it here. I'll buy you the damn cookbook."

"I can buy it."

"Not today, princess. Do you need one of those, too?" I point to the starfish.

"No, but I want one of these candles."

It takes her five minutes the choose the scent she likes best, and then another five to find that scent in the shell she wants. They all look the exact damn same to me, but she wants one that "opens to the left," whatever difference that makes.

By the time we return to my truck, she's added a box of fudge, a couple t-shirts, and a bottle of wine to the haul.

"Let's take all this stuff back to the house, shower, and go somewhere good for dinner."

"You want to eat again?"

"We've only eaten twice today."

"But we ate a lot both times."

"I might eat a lot the third time, too." I ease out of the parking spot. "And I might eat you for dessert."

"Not in the restaurant."

"Never say never."

She stretches her hand across the console to push a bite of fudge up to my mouth. I part my lips and let her feed it to me, and then I grab her fingers and suck them clean. She squirms in her seat. "I haven't washed my hands since lunch, you filthy animal."

"You wouldn't like me if I wasn't dirty."

"I might still like you. Probably not as much, though." She pops a piece of fudge into her own mouth and smiles.

Landry

SUNDAY MORNING, I'M AWAKENED by Vaughn's hand on my inner thigh. He woke me this way yesterday, too, and frankly, I could get used to being woken up like this every day. "Let me guess," I say. "You think we should eat breakfast before we head home."

"Oh, we're definitely doing that." His hand glides further up my leg until it grazes my bare pussy. "But I thought you might want to come before breakfast."

"Oh, I'm definitely doing that." I roll away from him. "But I have to pee first."

"Okay, but hurry. I'm starving."

I laugh all the way to the bathroom. He jokes, but honestly, I think he'd have been perfectly fine with doing nothing but eating and having sex this whole weekend. His eyes are on me as I walk back to the bed. "I swear, if men came with instructions, it'd be a short list: feed, fuck, repeat."

"That's not true." He lunges for me as soon I climb back into bed, pulling me on top of him. "We need water and sleep, too."

I sit up and straddle him, not moving to put him inside me yet. Thin curtains filter the early morning light. His lashes are unfairly long and dark. They fan out in a thick swoop from the outer corner of his eyelid, casting tiny shadows on the edge of his right cheekbone. I trace the feathery tips with my finger. He blinks rapidly and shakes his head. "That tickles."

"I didn't know you were ticklish."

"I'm not. But my eyelashes apparently are."

"Does this tickle?" I rock my pussy over the underside of his cock.

He pinches my nipples. "Does this?"

Lifting my hips, I take his erection in my hand and drag the head through my wet folds. "Does this?"

His thumb presses against my clit. "Does this?"

"I'm not sure. Move it around, tickle it some more."

He bucks his hips. "Slide that sweet pussy all the way down my cock. Go slow. Let me feel you stretching around me."

I slide down, and he keeps his thumb in place, allowing me to control the pressure as I sit lower.

"Yeah, that's my girl. That tight little snatch feels as good as it looks. Looks as good as it tastes." I rock up and back on him.

"There you go. Spill those sweet juices all over me. Make us both a mess."

"As if I could help it with you." His thumb circles over my clit. I lean into it for a few minutes before I sit back. "Let me do it," I say. He takes my hips in both hands but he doesn't guide me, just holds me steady while I grind my clit against his granite-hard cock and get myself off.

"The only thing better than watching you come undone with my dick inside you is feeling it happen." He flips us, gives me some space, and says, "Get on your knees. Spread your legs wide. Give me an open invitation."

I invite him to the fullest of my flexibility. And he wrecks me.

He kisses my neck between ragged breaths. "Shower together?"

"Yeah," I agree. "But let's hurry. I'm starving."

I like how easily I can make him laugh. I like a whole lot of things about him.

The parking garage at The Nouveau is quiet. Vaughn backs into his usual spot, and he insists on carrying both our packed bags. "You can carry those." He nods at the shopping bags. I know there's no point in arguing with him. His duffle is probably light compared to my weekender that I could barely zip after I repacked it this morning, but it wouldn't matter what they weighed or how many we had; he'd want to carry them all.

I'm trying to see that through his eyes: as chivalry and not chauvinism, but I've worked hard to carry my own weight in every sense of the word. Maybe someday I won't have to remind myself he's not trying to steal my independence every time he reaches to carry something for me.

My freshly wallpapered living room wall is the first thing I see when we step inside my apartment. "I love it even more in person. They did such a great job." The dark teal with silver veining makes my boring gray couch stand out, but it looks right now, like it's intentionally understated. Like it was chosen instead of settled for.

Vaughn kisses my forehead and quietly says, "Thank you."

"For what?"

"For letting me take care of that for you. You're not always easy to do things for."

"I know. I'm working on it."

I set my new candle on my used coffee table while he takes my bag to my room. I leave the cookbook on the kitchen counter because I'll be using that later, and then I open the fudge and divvy it up, putting half in a container for him to take. He laughs when he sees it. "You didn't have to do that."

"I don't need to eat all this fudge."

"You could've taken it to the office in the morning and shared it with Carina."

"I'll still be sharing my half with her."

Our goodbye kiss is a long one, and it's bittersweet. The fairytale of our weekend is over.

"How do you feel about the beach in winter?" Vaughn asks.

"Um, I'm not sure. I've never been in the winter."

"It's my favorite time to go, and I've got another weekend to cash in for the beach house. We'll go back when it's cold and make use of the fireplace."

"Why are you smiling at me like that?"

"I'm just admiring your cute little freckled nose."

"The sun fried your brain. Go home. Get some rest."

Watching him walk across my apartment to leave, I wonder about all the little things I don't know yet. Does he have a favorite color? Is it blue? What would he name a dog if he got one? "Hey, Vaughn."

He turns and smiles over his shoulder. "Yeah?"

"When's your birthday?"

"Christmas Day. I know how it feels to have it ignored."

It's too soon to be planning his birthday cake, but there goes my brain. I bet he likes basic chocolate cake with plain chocolate frosting. Uncomplicated, but heavy and sweet. The kind where the first bite is so rich it overwhelms your tastebuds, but before you know it, you've eaten the whole slice, and you know if you let yourself, you could eat the whole damn cake.

I dump all the clothes from my weekender into the washing machine. Some sand spills in with them. You can never get it all shaken out of your clothes, no matter how hard you try, but it doesn't frustrate me this time; it makes me laugh. I lean against the machine as it starts to fill and imagine cozying up in front of a fireplace at the beach with Vaughn.

Fuck, I honestly can't tell if I've just been exhaustively dicknotized, or if I'm falling stupid in love with him. Maybe it's still too soon to tell.

Maybe I don't want to know yet.

Vaughn

I stare in the mirror as I brush my teeth before I turn in for the night, but I can't even see myself there. All I can see is Landry, standing in the waves, laughing with the sun in her eyes and the breeze in her hair. So much for never being stupid over a woman again.

I'm fucking gone for this one.

Maybe I have been since the day I met her. Maybe I'm not kidding myself when I think we could be good together. Maybe.

So many maybes.

Fuuuuck me.

Landry

"You brought cupcakes and fudge? What are you trying to do to me?" Carina pretends to be appalled but she takes a cupcake.

"I didn't make the fudge, but the cupcakes are homemade. I've been searching for the perfect peanut butter frosting recipe forever, and I think this might be the one."

"Is the cupcake chocolate?"

"Banana."

"Even better." She takes a bite and her eyes roll back. "Are you kidding me? I want to lick this frosting off a dick."

Vonnie spins around the corner like a tornado. "Did somebody say we're licking frosting off dicks in here? Where do I get in line?"

"You've gotta try these cupcakes Landry made." Carina holds the container up so Vonnie can help herself. Lolita licks the air above them.

Vonnie holds one up to her nose. "Is this peanut butter frosting?" She takes a nibble. "Oh, sign me up for the dick licking! I'll go twice."

Vaughn halts in his tracks. "I can come back later."

"You want to come in here right now," Vonnie says. "And try one of these cupcakes our little sexpot manager has whipped up."

His smile is quick at her reference. "They're that good, huh?"

"They're amazing!" Carina sings my praises again.

He plays dumb. "What kind of frosting is this?"

"It's peanut butter!" Vonnie is astounded he didn't recognize it. She clearly bought his act. "And it's damn good." She turns to me. "Do you share your recipes? I have an old friend who absolutely adores a good peanut butter frosting, but trying to find a decent recipe for one is like trying to find a stiff cock in a convent."

"I got it from a new cookbook, and I'll be happy to make you a copy."

"Send me a screenshot," Carina says.

Autry strolls in to see what all the fuss is about. He takes one whiff of the cupcake Carina hands him and says, "Oh, my word. Is that peanut butter frosting I smell? I absolutely adore a good peanut butter frosting."

Wait a minute. Did he just . . . could he be . . .? I need to sit down. Carina has already collapsed to her chair. Vonnie floats out of the office without a single word to any of us. Vaughn's smiling wide at the possibility. Autry is lost in a haze of peanut butter and banana ecstasy. When the man finally speaks again, he simply says, "Ah, thanks for the memories, dear girl." He takes the rest of his cupcake to go.

Vaughn grabs a second on his way out. "Tell Holden to come get a cupcake," I yell before he rounds the corner. "Because I'm sure that one's not for him."

"I'm starving. I skipped breakfast."

There is no way that man skipped breakfast.

Carina takes a piece of fudge and closes the lid. When she sees the logo on the box, she says, "You went to Galveston this weekend? Who'd you go with?"

"Just me. I needed some beach therapy."

"Good for you. I should go to the beach more often."

"Well, it would be easier if you didn't have to work every Saturday. I think it's time we added a part-time leasing agent, Carina."

"Thanks. It would actually be nice to have some full weekends off again."

"Oh, thank goodness. I was worried you might be offended."

"No, it's time. I know you're not getting rid of me."

"Never."

"Okay, but when are you going to give yoga a try?"

"Way to ambush me when my guard's down." I laugh. "Is there a class tonight?"

"Seven-thirty. Vinyasa flow."

"I have no idea what that means, but give me the address and I'll meet you there."

Vaughn

I'M CROUCHED BY THE pantry when Holden enters the apartment. We don't have a high rate of tenant turnover, but, like any other place, when you enter a recently vacated unit for the first time, you never know what you'll find. "Look at this," I say. "I don't know what the hell kind of pet they had, but it ate half the damn baseboards."

"Rabbit," he says with confidence. "Saw it when I changed their air filters last month. It had a cage, but I don't think it spent much time in it."

"Great. Why can't anybody just get dogs and cats anymore? No, it's gotta be iguanas and ravens and shit."

"Whoa. Somebody here has a raven?"

"Sure. And when you get a chance, go meet the giraffe next door."

"Oh." He laughs. "You were joking about the raven."

"I hope so, but if one came flying through here, I probably wouldn't be shocked to see it."

He picks up a trim puller and starts loosening damaged baseboards by the door. In the kitchen, most of them have so little wood left, they'll have to be chiseled off. *Who keeps a rabbit cooped up in an apartment? Fucking assholes.*

"Does anybody actually have an iguana, though?"

"If there's only one iguana here, I'd be surprised."

"I wonder what the most exotic pet in the building is."

"If you were writing that detail into your screenplay, what would you make it?" I've learned if I can get him talking about his writing, he's a lot more productive. He gets going and he'll tell me all about it, riff off his own ideas. He'll stop every now and then to type a quick note in his phone, but he gets right back to work. He always thanks me, says it helps him to talk through plot problems. All I know is helps get the job at hand done.

"Maybe a monitor lizard." He pops the end of the board he's been working on from the wall.

"Do you know how damn big a monitor lizard gets?"

"Yeah, but they're not usually aggressive toward humans. And their bite's not fatal. They can do some damage, but they're not as bad as people make them out to be." He removes another board.

"Oh, good. I'll run out at lunch and get two."

"Did you know the platypus is venomous?"

"Well, scratch those little duck-billed fuckers off the list. What about a miniature hippopotamus? Would you give your character one of those?" I add to the pile of wood chips I've removed.

"No way, dude. Hippos are psycho. I wouldn't even trust a pygmy."

"I'll make a note. Trust no hippo."

"You know what miniature would be a cool pet?" he asks, hammering in the trim puller to start on a new section. "A Highland cow. Those little things are cute as hell, man. You couldn't have one in an apartment, but if you had a big enough yard. Did you know you can milk them? I bet Landry would get one of those if she could."

"Do you spend a lot of time wondering about what kind of pet Landry would get?"

"No. Not really." He shrugs. "She just seems like she'd have a whole farm full of miniature animals. Horses, donkeys, cows . . . hot-girl shit, right?"

Do not throw the hammer. Do not throw the hammer. "She's a grown woman, not a girl. Is she in your screenplay?"

"No. The female lead in my script gets railed too often. If I based her on Landry, I wouldn't be able to face her. I'd have to get a new job."

I white-knuckle the hammer grip. "Maybe you should give the female lead a little more agency."

"I can't believe you just used the word agency. You don't usually talk like that. But it's not like she gets assaulted or anything. She's just really into sex."

I lean forward and press my head against the wall for a few beats. "How about a peacock for that character? They always struck me as the sluts of the bird world."

"Actually, the saltmarsh sparrow is the most promiscuous bird in the world."

"That would definitely be an odd pet."

"Yeah. Maybe I don't need to add a unique pet, but a unique job. Like a scientist who studies the world's most promiscuous birds. That character might be into all kinds of weird shit."

"Your brain is into all kinds of weird shit."

"Dude, I'm a writer."

"Right now, you're a baseboard puller."

"Yeah, but I'm writing while I do it."

"I know." I drop another nail into a plastic cup. "So, is her unique job what gets her killed?"

"It could be. Somebody she interviews in her research could be the killer. Like some reclusive maniac who lives deep in the swamp where a rare bird is nesting, and he doesn't like anybody coming onto his property, so he threatens her, but she keeps coming back because she's too committed to her work to prioritize her own safety."

"Would you really make him the killer or just use him to mislead the audience?"

"You're right. The real killer should be someone nobody would suspect. Like her landlord, who's always coming around and being helpful, but he's secretly obsessed with her."

"Secret obsessions never lead to anything good."

"This is why I love working with you. It's like I'm workshopping while I'm working."

"Glad I can help."

He's pulling baseboards like a machine. The faster his brain spins, the faster his hands work. Hell, I halfway want to read this damn screenplay when it's done.

"How's it going?" Landry pokes her head in the door. "Holden stopped in the office on his way out to see if there were any cupcakes left. He said a rabbit ate half the walls in here?"

"It only ate the trim."

She looks around at the buckets full of broken and chewed boards and nods. "They chew so much because their teeth never stop growing."

"What is it with your generation and random animal facts?"

"We took a lot of tests. Our brains were programmed to capture anything that seemed like it might show up on a test someday. We literally grew up frantically taking mental screenshots of random facts. We have folders in our heads full of them. It's why we kick ass at trivia."

"Did you know the saltmarsh sparrow is the most promiscuous bird in the world?"

"Dude, just look at human porn like a normal person."

I do a spit take with my water. She caught me completely unprepared with that one. "Do you watch porn?"

Her gaze drops. "Sometimes. Most people do."

"What kind do you watch?"

"The kind with no birds."

"Well, damn. I guess things aren't going to work out between us then." I could listen to her laugh all day. "Seriously, what do you like to watch."

"Pretty basic stuff."

"Multiple partners?"

"If it's porn, there will likely be multiple partners on screen at some point. But I don't want to do that in real life."

"I'm not suggesting we do anything. I'm just curious about you. I think there are some kinks lurking beneath the surface that you haven't uncovered yet. And maybe some that you're aware of, but haven't experimented with much."

"Hit me those. The ones you think I'm aware of."

"Spanking."

"That's been hard to experiment with since my divorce. Hard to reconcile liking that."

I motion for her to come into the kitchen. I lift her onto the island and sit on the counter across from her. "Yeah, but you do like it, and that's okay."

"With you, yeah."

"Nothing is good with someone you don't trust. Erotic spanking is a pretty average kink."

"Don't call me average. What else have you got on me?"

"Exhibitionism."

"Hard no. I don't want strangers to watch me have sex."

"But you like the thrill of being somewhere we might get caught."

"Yeah, but everybody probably likes that."

"Probably not everybody." I shake my head and smile. "But I like it a lot."

"I don't even think you would care if we got caught."

"For myself, no. I don't ever want you to be in an uncomfortable situation, though." I take a drink from my water bottle and offer it her. She shakes me off. "But I think your exhibitionism might run a little deeper than you're ready to acknowledge. I'm not pushing you to try anything you don't want, but if that changes, you can tell me."

"And then what? We'll go to Whole Foods and have sex in the bakery?"

"Well, not at Whole Foods. Those people are way too uptight. Maybe H-E-B."

Her jaw drops. "I'm not fucking you at H-E-B like a commoner. You better come up with a better place than that."

"Have you ever been to a club?"

"Yes, I've been to plenty of clubs." She starts to roll her eyes but they stop at the mid-point. "Oh, you meant a club where sex is supposed to happen there."

"Yeah, that kind of club."

"Do you go to that kind of club a lot?"

"No, but I've been to a few. They can be fun. If you ever wanted to check one out, I'd take you. It can be a safe place to experiment."

"Okay. And if I never want to go?"

"Then we never will."

"What about you?"

"I'd go with you or not at all. It's not a regular day-in-the-life thing for me either. I just want you to know you can be open with me. About anything."

"But when you do go . . . what above average kinks are you into there?"

"I think I'm pretty average, too. It would be fun to observe with you."

"Is that allowed? Can you go as a spectator?"

"Well, they won't give you a badge that says that, but you don't have to participate in anything."

"What would you want to participate in?"

"I wouldn't mind bending you over a spanking bench in front of other people. I don't think you'd entirely mind it either." She shifts on the counter. I think she's every bit as turned on by the thought as I am, but I won't press her to tell me one way or the other.

"Would you want other people to touch me?"

"No." I rake my hand through my hair. "I'm very below average on that. I don't like to share. Which I guess brings up the point that we haven't officially said what we are to each other. I'm not seeing anybody else."

"I'm not either. And for the record, I don't think that makes you below average."

"I don't want to see anybody else."

"Me either."

"Okay, so, I guess we're officially a couple." I knew we needed to have this conversation but I didn't realize how palpable it would be when the weight lifted.

"But a secret couple," she says.

Disappointment is not the expression I want to see on her face right now.

"Only here. Unless you want to keep it a secret from your friends and family, too."

"I want to tell the whole world about you. Us. But we can't."

"We can tell the people who matter." I hop down from the counter and bridge the space between us. "Right now, I think we should fuck for the first time as a couple."

"We've been a couple. The officialness is a technicality."

"And I technically want to fuck you."

"Spank me first?"

"What are you trying to do, get me to buy you a miniature cow?"

"Wait. Has that been an option this whole time?"

"Take your clothes off, gorgeous."

Landry

I'M NOT SURE IF it's from being bent over the island in the rabbit hutch apartment or my first yoga class, but it's been three days since both those events, and my hamstrings still hate me.

"You need to come to another yoga class and work out that soreness," Carina says for the third time today. But who's counting?

Vaughn has his own list of positions he swears will help. "How am I this sore? I work out. It's like yoga woke up muscles that have been asleep my whole life."

"It'll do that. But the more you come, the more flexible you'll get."

"Please don't say that in front of—" I stop myself before I say his name.

She smiles. "I won't."

"I got in touch with the woman who lives in 708."

"Is she going to be able to catch up her rent?" She grimaces ahead of my response.

I shake my head. "No. Her boyfriend moved out. Apparently, he was paying the bulk of the bills. She said she'd be out by this weekend."

"Why do women put themselves in that position?"

"Because they think it'll never happen to them."

"Yeah, I guess you're right," she says. "We let ourselves believe a lot of things can't happen to us."

"I've got a conference call with the owners this afternoon. They're not going to be happy to hear we've got a broken lease with back rent due. Losses happen, but these owners are penny counters." I refill my coffee, hoping to fortify with caffeine before that conversation has to take place.

"They'll give you the standard 'we bought this place to make money, not lose it' speech, as if you caused it, but then they'll move on to the next topic and let their attorney handle the broken lease."

"Pursuing legal action will cost more in attorney fees than what she owes."

"The attorneys are on a retainer," Carina reminds me. "They cost the same, no matter what."

I knew that. But I always have a soft spot for women who get stuck. "We have a waiting list, though. It's not like we can't fill the unit immediately."

"But we can't bill a new tenant for a previous tenant's past-due balance."

"Yeah, I know." I'm softer than usual about this one, and I'm not sure why. I've been softer than usual a lot lately. When my life was at its worst, I never wished the same on other people, never wanted anyone else to have to share in my misery. But now that things are going great for me, I want great things for everyone. I used to be at least a little hard around the edges; now, I'm a complete fucking marshmallow. That's not exactly great for certain aspects of my job.

"Oh, my gosh! This is exactly what you need!" Carina says.

"A life coach?"

"A new Yin Yoga class. It's like deep stretching. The first session is tonight at seven. I'll go with you." Her fingernails peck at her screen, and I know she's signing us both up. "Why would you need a life coach? You have your shit together better than anybody your age should have a right to."

If she only knew. "Thanks."

"Therapy, on the other hand, is for everyone."

"You believe in crystals and therapy?"

"Why would they be exclusive of one another?"

"Magic versus science?" I offer.

"Crystals aren't magic. They're spiritual. And therapy is a soft science, so trust me, there's room for both."

"I love the way you look at the world."

"There's no point in letting it make you hard."

"Sometimes hard is good."

"Only for dicks."

We both laugh and look to door to see if Vonnie responds to her call signal. "You said dicks and she didn't appear."

"Should we call and check on her?"

As if on cue, Lolita slithers past the office door. Carina starts to get up, but Vonnie is right behind her. She picks up her snake, gives us a wave. She's singing about peanut butter. "You made up another song?" I ask.

Vonnie stomps into the office. "I'll have you know that is a real song, sung by the great Chubby Checker."

Carina cocks her head. "Is that a real person?"

"Do you hear these two, Lolly? Clueless, clueless girls." She bounces out of the office, singing about peanut butter again.

"Okay, I have to know," I say.

"I'm already looking it up."

"Is it a real song?"

"Unbelievably, yes." she sets her phone on her desk and lets it play.

We listen to the whole silly song twice. By the second time, it's impossible not to sing along, and it's impossible to be upset about much of anything. Vaughn passes the office, stops, and backs up. He listens for a few seconds like he's not sure he's hearing the words right, shakes his head once he's confirmed it, and walks off.

That spontaneous dose of silliness destroyed whatever funk was creeping in on me. It could come back, but at the moment, I'm good.

The Nouveau is owned by a property management corporation. The corporation has three owners: a husband and wife, James and Angela, and another man, Weldon, who honestly, seems to be the voice of reason every time I talk to them. He intervenes when Angela starts the expected rant about losing money over the broken lease. When the husband tries to pile on in his wife's defense, Weldon cuts him off, too.

Normally, I'd say it was strange for all the owners to be on every call and micromanage at this level, but that's how this group operates. Thank goodness it's not just James and Angela. They make sure to state their opinion that we could've held off for a while on the new garage door. Weldon speaks up in support of replacing it when we did. He throws out out some legalese about assumed liability and staying competitive with comparable properties. I don't have to see their resumes to know he has substantially more industry experience than his partners.

I'd much prefer to deal with Weldon only, but so far, that hasn't happened. I thought it might've been because I was new, but Carina says she can't imagine James and Angela letting a single decision be made without their input. She knows them better than I do.

I leave the Yin Yoga class feeling brand new, not a hint of soreness left in my body. It wasn't the kind of stretching I expected, but holding those gentle poses worked. Great. Not only am I a marshmallow, but I might be turning into a yoga girl, too.

My shower didn't leave me as drained as I expected. I feel energized, but I can't be up all night.

Me: *Want to come over? I have some of that peanut butter frosting left in the fridge.*

Vaughn: *You don't need a spoonful of frosting to tempt me.*

Me: *I wasn't planning to eat it off a spoon.*

Vaughn: *On my way.*

Carina was on to something with this whole frosted dick idea. Straight from the bowl, it's cold and thick, but within seconds of making contact with his warm skin, it softens and becomes easily spreadable. I use my fingers to coat his length, obscuring the prominent veins, and then letting my tongue expose them again.

If I have a sugar high when I'm done, it'll be worth it to have felt the way he's shuddering as I lick and lave. He holds my hair back and watches me frost him and lick him clean, stopping short of the tip, withholding attention from the swell of his head just yet.

I have a bowl of warm water and a washcloth within reach because I'm not going to make him come with my mouth, and he's not putting anything sugar-coated inside my vagina. I'm here for a good time, not a yeast infection. His dick lurches when I make a third pass with the frosting, so I lavish the crown with a few wide strokes of my tongue before I reach for the warm cloth and clean him. He groans at being denied the chance to come, but he doesn't hate having me wipe him down like this.

Before I stand to kiss him, I scoop more of the frosting, cover my nipples, and lick my fingers clean. He pulls me to my feet and kisses me hard, careful not to press his body to mine and wipe away the frosting from my nipples.

When he's ready, he licks and sucks the peanut butter confection from one stiff peak and then the other. He pushes me down on the bed and fucks me like it's been weeks since we've seen each other.

He's got me practically folded in half, my knees at my shoulders. My hamstrings don't resist in the slightest; my whole body is putty under him, pliable and compliant with whatever position he wants it to hold.

After he releases me, I go to the bathroom to clean myself while he recovers on my bed. I pause as I return, standing naked, watching him looking at me like he's amazed by the image of my body in the doorway—an ordinary body he's seen so many times by now, but still, he looks at me in that way. "Think you might want to show me that club this weekend?"

"If you still want to see it when the weekend comes, that's exactly what I want to do. If you change your mind, we'll see it whenever."

We'll see it this weekend.

Vaughn

SHE ASKED TO GO. *It's going to be fine.* I increase the incline on my treadmill and run faster.

What's the worst that could happen? We go inside, she hates it, and wants to leave? That's fine. We'll leave. We go inside, she loves it, and wants to play? Great. We'll play. We go inside, she loves it, and decides she wants to play with someone else? Not happening. *It could happen, asshole. You better fucking think about it.*

When she asked if I wanted to share her, I said no, but I didn't ask her how she felt about it. *Because assuming she agreed with you was easier. Asshole.*

I could ask her tonight before we go, but honestly, how can I expect her to know how she feels when she's never been in that situation before? She might think she knows how she feels, but that could change once she's inside and shit gets real. All the conventions of the outside world fall away when you're there in a dimly lit space with brave bodies and erotic energy buzzing all around you—not to mention the literal buzz of alcohol if you add that into the mix.

What if she gets drunk on the freedom of it all and wants to try things she never would've imagined? How am I going to know what she'll be glad she was bold enough to try versus what she might regret? *She doesn't need you to know. She's a grown woman. She can make her own decisions. This was all your idea, asshole.*

Sweat runs into my eyes. I run harder.

When the shower spray goes cold, I turn the handle twice to chase the last drops of hot water before I get out.

Dark jeans, white button down, brown boots . . . I still clean up well. On the outside, anyway. I'm ready for dinner wherever she chooses.

And I'm ready for whatever she chooses after, too.

Landry

VAUGHN TAKES MY BREATH away when I open my door. Nice jeans and a pressed white shirt. Those full-quill ostrich boots didn't come cheap. He doesn't always give off that stereotypical Texas vibe, which is good because I don't always like it, but I'm liking the hell out of it right now.

He looks like he could own this whole place. He could own me for a while.

"You look great," I say.

"You look like I might need to go back across the hall and get a jacket."

"It's too hot out for a jacket. You look fine without one."

"I meant for you."

"This dress is not that revealing." I spin in my only little black dress. "Actually, you've seen me in this dress before. It's the same one I was wearing when Jenna and I ran into you on our way out."

"Yeah, and I thought you needed a jacket over it then, too." He smiles and kisses my forehead to be sure I know he's teasing. Mostly, anyway. "What are you in the mood for?"

What would I not be in the mood for with him looking like he does right now? It's clear he's asking what I want for dinner, but that doesn't stop my mind from entertaining a few sexual possibilities for a moment before I answer. "Probably nothing too heavy."

"So, steak then. Perfect."

We were obviously going to a steakhouse, regardless, or at least unless I specified something else. I won't be eating a steak, but I don't object.

A martini works to take the edge off the tension that's had me its grip all day, but I refuse a second because I don't want to be too at ease when we go to the club. Plus, I'm dining light, so no drinking heavy.

"Are you eating that chicken or just pushing it around on your plate?"

"I ate a lot of it. It was a whole breast."

"Oh, no. Not a whole one." He takes the final bite of his steak, wipes his mouth on the cloth napkin from his lap and drops it next to his glass. His whiskey's nearly gone, too, but like me, he only had one.

It's nice to never have to worry if he'll have one too many and get volatile. He always stays in control. Dependable, but never boring. Sometimes, I wonder what he'd be like if he let go just a little more, but I'm not sure he can. He never sits with his back to the door. His peripheral vision never goes unchecked for long. I see his eyes sweep the room from time to time, and not just in restaurants; he's hypervigilant everywhere.

But when I talk, he listens, genuinely pays attention. He's never looking past me; he's looking at me.

He knows it's a given I'm skipping dessert. Even if we weren't headed where we are when we leave here, I'd have skipped it tonight. I've eaten sugar every day this past week, whether it was a cupcake, candy, or a quick bite of frosting straight from the fridge. Or a not-so-quick helping of frosting, not from a spoon.

The club is only a ten-minute drive away. I didn't realize how close it was, and I still want to go, but I wish it was ten minutes farther. He pulls into the parking lot, severing my anticipation on one level while it ramps up on another.

"Hey," he reaches over and tucks a section of my hair behind my ear. "If you change your mind at any point and want to leave—"

"I know." I touch his hand at my temple. "Thank you for making sure I understand we don't have to stay, but I've done all my soul searching and research. I'm good."

His smile is uneasy.

"Are you okay with this?" I ask. He's spent so much time making sure I know what to expect and that I'm okay, it never occurred to me he might have some reservations of his own.

"I'm excited because I want to introduce you to whatever you're interested in, but I can't help but worry about you being uncomfortable and not saying anything."

"I promise you, if I am uncomfortable, I will tell you. I'm not afraid that you'll get mad, and I don't feel obligated in any way to be here. I want to know what it's like."

"All right. Then, I guess we're doing this."

His lips are soft and reassuring, but until I get through my first visit—maybe my only visit—I know my stomach is going to stay warm and jumpy.

He reaches for his door handle. "Duck!" he says, suddenly using his hand at the back of my head to assist me in doing just that.

My head is beneath the dash, but I didn't see anything. I have no idea what I'm taking cover from. "What is it? What's happening?"

"I'm not sure." He shakes his head, crouching down next to me, but not so low that he can't peer over the dash. "There's no way I'm seeing this."

"What are you seeing?"

"You're not going to believe me unless you see it with your own eyes. Lift up slowly, just enough to tell me I'm not hallucinating."

I tentatively raise my head a few inches and look through partially closed eyes as if I might be about to see something traumatizing. "Holy fuck!" My eyes couldn't get any more open.

"Or unholy."

"Are they coming or going?"

"They're leaving."

"And you're sure they're together?"

"What do you think the odds are that they ran into each other here, Landry?"

"But Vonnie and Autry? At a sex club? Together?"

"Well, that's who we're looking at and that's where we are, so, yeah."

"Do you think they . . . ?"

"I'm trying really hard not to think about that."

"You know what, though? This could actually make sense." I lift up a few more inches, and Vaughn gently pulls me back down. "I think Vonnie really misses performing. She's for sure an exhibitionist. Maybe she performs for him in there. Do you think he used to go to her shows back in the day?"

Vaughn smiles. "Anything's possible."

"Vonita Viper strikes again. But why doesn't she just dance for him in her apartment? Or his?"

"Maybe it had to be a secret back when he started watching her, and they never changed it."

"And maybe they pretended to hate each other back then to keep anyone from getting suspicious," I add.

"They fell into roles they can't step out of. Or don't want to."

"Ooh, that's an interesting angle." I'm feeling borderline giddy about this discovery now. "Maybe that's part of the fun for them."

"They definitely don't really hate each other."

I lift up again. "Oh, my God, they're canoodling!" I squeeze his bicep. "That's the cutest, sweetest thing ever."

"They're doing what?"

"Shut up. Just let them live."

He laughs and tugs me back down out of view. I can't help myself; I keep popping up like a damn meerkat.

"I'm glad you're enjoying this. They're getting in their separate cars."

"She brought her own car? So clandestine. It's freaking adorable. Like a movie. I guess they don't let her bring Lolita here."

"Probably not." His head turns and I know he's watching them drive off. "They're gone. You can sit up."

I try, but I can't bring myself to sit any higher than a slouch, just in case I have to hit the deck again. "Of all the unexpected things I tried to prepare myself for, that wasn't even on my radar."

"If it had been, I'd be worried. Do you still want to go inside?"

"We may as well at this point." I shrug. "What bigger surprise could we find?"

"Please don't tempt fate like that."

"I wonder if they're regulars."

"Let's stop wondering things about them altogether."

"I can *pretend* to do that."

"Good enough for me."

He takes my hand in the parking lot. On the bright side, seeing Vonnie and Autry has obliterated most of my anxiety about this place. But what if I enjoy this experience and want to come back? It's bad enough we have to sneak around The Nouveau, but having to look over our shoulders at a sex club might kill the vibe. Or would it make everything twice as exciting?

I squeeze his hand. "I just had a thought that I think might confirm my exhibitionism kink before we even cross the threshold."

"If it had anything to do with the two people we just saw, please keep it to yourself. My kinks have limits."

We enter the club, hand in hand and laughing. This is off to a much different start than I could've ever imagined. The entry process holds no surprises. I learned most of what to expect from the online application, but I'd forgotten they require you to turn in your phone. We put them in the same basket and watch as a woman shuts them into a small locker. She gives us a key on a stretchy bracelet. Vaugh asks if I want to hold onto it, and I don't know why, but having the key makes me feel more at ease about giving up my phone.

A large man scans us with a handheld wand, and then we're free to pass through the solid double doors that lead into the main room. There are tables and booths, two bars, and a dance floor. At this point, it looks like any other club. No sexual acts are allowed to take place out here, including masturbation. It's just music and people, some less clothed than others, but nothing more than conversation and dancing is happening.

We get drinks and stand at a high-top table near the bar. A couple approaches us and stops. The man looks like he's probably about ten years older than Vaughn, but the woman appears to be closer to my age, both tanned and dark-haired. She smiles and compliments my necklace while the guy whispers something to Vaughn, who shakes his head no. They walk away.

"Did he just ask if we wanted to have sex with them?"

"That was the gist of it." He takes a sip of whiskey. "I assume I answered correctly?"

"Yes." A song comes on that I haven't heard since high school, and I automatically bob my head. "So, the other rooms are all down that hallway?" I gesture with my glass.

"Yeah, but we can stay out here as long as you want. We never have to go back there at all."

"I know." Two women reenter the main room from the hallway. They're wearing dresses, but no shoes, laughing, and walking so close together their arms are touching. Seems safe to assume they just played together in some capacity. I watch one couple go toward the back rooms as another pair walks away from them. Some people smile and nod at each other, while others look straight ahead.

We get propositioned again, but this time, the woman approaches me instead. I respond the same way Vaughn did, and they move on. "I guess that's going to keep happening."

"Doesn't matter. They're not offended."

I slam the rest of my drink, which was far more than a shot's worth. "Do you want to go down the hall?"

"If you do."

"I do."

He takes my hand, and that small casually intimate act makes me feel like we belong, both here and to each other. When we reach the entrance to the hallway, he releases my hand and places his at the small of my back to guide me.

We pass two unoccupied rooms, both with king-sized beds, one with safari-themed bedding, and the next done all in black. The doors are wide open so we know before we reached the viewing windows whether anyone is in there or not, but then we reach an open door on a room that is most definitely occupied.

I nervously glance to my right, not ready to look in a more direct way. The room is dimly lit and everything is red, including the paint on the walls. The whole room is awash in a crimson glow that makes me think the lightbulbs may be red as well. All I can make out about the three people on the bed is their outlines. We slow at the viewing window, but don't come to a complete stop.

There is a room with a closed door and shut blinds on the window. It's not empty, but whatever is happening in there is for their eyes only. Total privacy is an option, just not the most popular.

And then we come to a room that matches my first mental image of a sex club. The door is open. It's a more communal space. There is no bed, but no shortage of equipment: the proverbial spanking bench Vaughn has referenced, a sex swing, and a few black pleather couches. Naked or partially naked bodies are plentiful. On one of the couches, it's hard to tell where one body ends and another begins. These scenes are playing out right before my eyes, but seeing it doesn't confirm anything for me.

Will I want to participate at some point? I still have no idea. All I know is not right now.

The only room I feel certain about is the final one, the room with cages, a stockade, wall restraints, and a whole display of whips and other implements. I know from my research that this club is considered pretty vanilla in the grand scheme of things, but the things in this room are all way outside my comfort zone. The room's not unoccupied though.

So many varied kinks being openly explored so close together. People gravitate to what they want and don't seem at all concerned about what's down the hall, or even on the next couch.

We aren't the only people strolling the hallway. I'm probably not the only newbie here tonight, but I feel like everyone who looks at me instantly knows. I slow when we get back to the room with the bench and couches. A woman bends over the bench, and unlike the one before her who wasn't restrained, a man fastens cuffs around her wrists. There's something kind of hot, but also kind of not about that to me. I imagine being her, and I'm not appalled. I'm surprisingly neutral on a lot of what I'm seeing. Not appalled, but not called.

We head back to the bar. A couple comes over and strikes up a conversation. No whispered invitations pass between us, just some mild, fully-clothed flirtations. This is kind of fun. Mingling is more comfortable now, but when we finish our drinks and Vaughn asks if I'm ready to go, I say yes.

He waits until we're in his truck to ask what I think.

Staring at the building, the fact that we even went in there feels unreal, like maybe it didn't really happen. I thought it would feel more momentous somehow. So much to process. "Is it weird that I'm not exactly sure what I think?"

"No, not at all."

"Is it weird that I think if we came back again, I still might not be sure?"

"No. We can come back as often as you want or never again, but whatever you want or don't want, or feel or don't feel will never be weird."

My stomach quivers, but it's a different type of precariousness than when we arrived. I like this feeling, knowing that we have a new secret thing. It doesn't matter that nothing happened. "Take me home and fuck me like you definitely do not hate me."

"That's the only way I ever could." His kiss turns me on more than all the things I witnessed tonight combined. But I undoubtedly felt some additional warmth between my legs a few times, and he is rock-fucking-hard right now.

Vaughn

The week's half over and not one tenant has made me want to get out crayons to explain something. Hell, Holden hasn't even annoyed me with his unsolicited animal facts. And he just showed up right on time again. All in all, the guy's a hard worker. I should probably go easier on him.

"How's the screenplay going? You figure out who the killer is yet?"

"I had some breakthroughs over the weekend. I've reworked a lot of it, like instead of having the woman have an unusual job, she's a successful real estate agent now. And I added a romantic subplot. She's secretly dating a plumber. He's definitely not the killer but it adds some good sexual tension to balance the suspense."

"A real estate agent and a plumber, huh? Interesting choices. How'd you come up with those jobs?"

"I don't know. It just came to me. And they fit so well with the whole opposites attract thing. It's a classic trope."

"The jobs people hold don't necessarily make them opposites."

"Yeah, but people love to see a refined woman with a crude guy. It bodes well for the everyman. If a dirty plumber can pull a hot woman in heels on the screen, the average male viewer feels hopeful about his own chances. And when a muscular blue-collar guy rescues and protects the leading lady, the average female viewer sees herself in the fairytale."

"Did somebody actually teach you that shit in a screenwriting class?" I pull harder than I mean to and send a splintered baseboard flying across the room.

"There's a lot more psychology that goes into screenwriting than most people realize."

Drop the fucking hammer. "I try really hard not to give you life advice, but you are fast approaching an age where youth no longer excuses ignorance. Every pretty woman you see is not a goddamn damsel in distress. They are not always in need of being rescued, not by a dirty plumber or anybody else."

"I'm telling you, man, it's a character dynamic that works."

"Jesus fuck! If you're writing porn, maybe! That's the only time a dirty plumber and a hot, helpless real estate agent might be all you need. But you seriously need to give your characters a little more depth." I stand up, and fight the urge to throw a cup of nails at the wall. "I need some fresh air. Make some progress on that wall while I'm gone."

I slam the door on my way out, reopen it, and stick my head back into the apartment. "And for record, I'm a licensed electrician, not a plumber!"

"Okay. But I'm not writing about you."

"You're sure as hell not! I need to read this script before you do anything with it." I slam the door again, but this time I actually leave, go upstairs, and lace up my running shoes. I need more than fresh air; I need hard ground under my feet.

Landry

VAUGHN SHOWS UP IN the office at closing time to tell me we have a unit that's being used as a grow house. "Nobody's living in that apartment, I can promise you. It's packed with nothing but tables, grow lights, and hydroponics. It was set up fairly recently. There's no mold on the sheetrock yet, but it wouldn't be long before it started. They had the thermostat at eighty degrees."

"How'd you discover it?"

"The guy who lives in the unit next door flagged me down. You can't smell it from the hallway yet, but it's unmistakable in his bathroom. He said he was sure nobody was living in the unit, and he was right. They've mostly got seedlings but there are few sizeable plants in there."

"That is the last thing I would think someone would use one of our apartments for."

"Just because they're enterprising doesn't mean they're smart."

Carina sighs. "I'll call the cops. We'll have to file a report. The good news is they'll dismantle it for us because they'll confiscate everything."

"What the hell is wrong with people?" I ask.

"In this case, stupidity," Vaughn says. "Are you heading upstairs?"

"Well, not now. I have to stay and handle this."

"No, you don't," Carina says. "I've got it. I was going to hang out to kill time before yoga, anyway."

"Okay. If you need me, give me a call." I grab my purse.

"All right. If you change your mind about going to yoga tonight, come back down."

When the elevator opens on our floor, Vaughn says, "Come hang out with me for a while. You seem stressed."

"You seem stressed."

"All the more reason for you to hang out with me."

I crowd Vaughn as he tries to get his key in the lock, rubbing my body against his to further complicate his efforts. I'm giving him a taste of his own medicine, not that he minds it, aside from not being able to get the door open.

"Are you really this anxious to get inside my apartment or are you just trying to make my life hard?"

"I'm trying to make something hard."

"Mission accomplished." He tries to kiss me, but I put my hand up to block him. "Whoa. Mixed signals," he teases.

"We're on camera, remember?"

"You like being on camera." He pulls me in front of him and pins me against his door. "And the camera loves you. And I don't think a kiss is going to look worse than you grinding on me."

"Grinding is an exaggeration. Vaughn, seriously, stop." Neck kisses are an unfair move right now. He shouldn't want to weaken my defenses here, but he always wants to do that. Always wants to win.

"Are you smiling for the camera?" His tongue traces the shell of my ear.

"I'm not smiling." Not for the camera, anyway, but trying to bite it back is impossible.

"Really?" He claims my wrists and presses them to the door over my head, resting his forehead on mine. "Because that looks like—"

The roof access door suddenly swings open, and voices spill out from the short stairwell into the hallway. Shit! How did we not hear someone coming? Vaughn doesn't jerk away from me; he stills as if to protect me.

No one other than the two of us has access to the roof. I'm afraid to look, but when I shift my eyes in that direction, I'm quickly reminded that no, we are not the only ones who have access to restricted spaces at The Nouveau. I'd rather it be intruders breaking into the building than who it really is.

The owners—all three looking at me looking at them. They freeze. We freeze. Time itself freezes.

There is no way to spin this into something innocent. Vaughn's hips are still pressed against me. Our faces are inches apart. He has my wrists captured and pinned.

Angela's performative gasp sucks all the oxygen from the air.

They've only been to the property once since I became the manager, and they let me know ahead of time they were coming. Vaughn didn't want to take a break to meet them that day, but I insisted. If only I'd left well enough alone, they wouldn't recognize him. He'd just be some guy in their eyes right now. But I've never been good at leaving well enough alone. And he's way more than just some guy at this point.

He releases my wrists and stands up straight. A surge of anger courses through me. Why are they here?

"Hi." I manage to keep my voice flat, unaffected. "Clearly, we didn't realize anyone was on the roof."

"Yes, well, we do happen to own it," Angela says. James steps forward and places a hand on his wife's shoulder. I can't tell if he's sending her a warning to stay calm or if it's a show of solidarity.

Weldon looks as if he's battling a smile. But why would he be smiling when he's just caught two employees breaking company policy? Maybe I've read him wrong all along and he's a sadist who gets off on ruining people's lives.

"Of course, you own it," I say. "You own the whole building. But you don't own me. If you're expecting an apology, I won't give you one because I'm not sorry. And if that costs me my job, I'll find another one."

Vaughn takes my hand. "You can't fire one of us and not the other."

"Mom? Dad? What the hell are y'all doing here tonight?" Carina's voice is jarring. I didn't even hear the elevator.

Wait. What the fuck did she just say? "These are your parents?"

"Two of them are." She glares at James and Angela. "You can't do this again. You can't keep losing good people because of that stupid nonfraternization policy!"

Weldon clears his throat. "We did away with that policy if I'm not mistaken. If y'all had these two sign it after our discussion . . ."

"We didn't make them sign it," James clarifies.

"Although it certainly appears we should have." Angela's words drip with condescension.

Her disgusted snarl is about to make me show my roots. She better wipe it off her face. Vaughn squeezes my hand as if he can sense the shift in me.

"So, there's not actually a non-fraternization policy?" he asks.

"Was anyone going to tell me that?" Carina demands. "Or is it still in place, but only for me? After all, it was established just for me."

"For your protection, Carina," Angela says.

"We wanted better for you," James adds.

Weldon sighs. "And none of that matters at the moment because the policy is gone. Landry, Vaughn, we're sorry to have interrupted your evening. We're leaving."

Vonnie and Autry round the corner together. "Well, well, well, she says. Are we having a hall party?" She doesn't have Lolita around her waist. Hopefully, that means she's in her habitat and not slithering freely.

"Miss Vonita and I were each taking our own walk," Autry explains. "Our paths crossed, and I felt it was best if she didn't walk unaccompanied this late in the evening." It's so damn cute that he keeps up their act. He has no idea we saw them earlier, or that his explanation doesn't even make sense because she's not walking out on the street. Appearances are everything to him, but not because he's an asshole like Angela, who just can't keep her damn mouth shut.

"This situation will need to be addressed, regardless of policy," she says.

"Wow. Why is everybody in the hall?" Holden looks from one face to the next.

Vaughn's grip tightens on my hand. "What the hell are you doing back here?"

Holden holds out a stack of papers fastened together with a binder clip. "I brought you a copy of my screenplay. It's not done yet, but your feedback always helps. Sometimes, a lay perspective is best. And you said you wanted to read it, so I thought . . ." His eyes zero in on my hand in Vaughn's. "Ooooooh, shit, dude. Your reaction to the plumber actually makes sense now! You thought I was writing about a plumber having a thing with Landry."

"Do the two of you just flaunt your affair to everyone in the building?" Angela asks. "With no regard for decorum at all? Policy aside, professionalism remains a requirement. And going forward—"

Vaughn's head turns swiftly toward the owners, and voice comes out calm and commanding as he cuts Angela off. "If any of you has a problem with the way I do my job, you feel free to let me know. But going forward, when it comes to my personal life, you can all three feel free to mind your own fucking business."

"My sentiments exactly." I step closer to him.

Weldon puts his hands up defensively. "Whoa, whoa, whoa. I think we've all gotten a little carried away here. This is neither the time nor the place. We'll schedule a meeting when calmer heads can prevail."

Angela opens her mouth to argue, but James steers her around us. The three of them walk toward the elevator. Vonnie and Autry have disappeared. Vaughn takes the script from Holden, who is the only person in this hallway with a smile on his face. "See you Monday," he says before he runs to catch the elevator.

As soon as he's out of sight, I look to Carina. She's shaken, but she's trying hard not to let it show. "I came up to let you know the police couldn't guarantee they'd be here before I left. They're going to text you when they show up so you can open the apartment for them."

"Okay," I say. "Do you have time to come in and sit with us? Maybe explain some things?"

"Sure."

Vaughn opens his door and the three of us enter his apartment and settle ourselves on his enormous couch. He cracks open beers. Carina hesitates, but then she takes one, says she's not really in the mood for yoga now, anyway. "I'm sorry I had y'all believing you had to sneak around. I swear I thought they would fire you. They did it before. I had no idea it was no longer a policy."

"I just don't understand why you're a leasing agent if your parents own this place," I say.

"It's not what they want, trust me. They want me to work directly with them, and learn to take over their portfolio some-day." She tips her bottle back. "I'd rather flip burgers than work side-by-side with my mother. I worked for her once. I never intended to do it again."

Vaughn nods. "Then why are you working for her now?"

"They didn't own The Nouveau when I started working here. They'd never owned a property like this. They always had rental houses and a couple small apartment buildings. Then they partnered with Weldon and bought this place."

"Did they buy it because you worked here?"

"To be fair, they were in the market for a luxury midrise. But I worked for them before, managing one of their apartment buildings." She takes a long pull from her beer. "I started dating one of the guys who worked on the landscaping crew. He was attractive and funny and nice, but they couldn't have their daughter dating 'a guy who pushes a lawnmower for a living.'" She throws air quotes up when she says it. "He was going to school to become a landscape architect, but they didn't want to know about his ambition. They just wanted him gone. So, they immediately implemented a non-fraternization policy."

"It doesn't work like that," Vaughn says. "You can't make a policy retroactive."

"No, but you can enforce it going forward. We kept dating for a while, but my parents found out, of course. And instead of firing me, they fired the landscaping company. His boss found out why and fired him. And then he stopped talking to me. Who could blame him?"

"That's why you didn't want to be the manager here," I say.

"I've been telling myself I was going to find another job ever since they became the owners, but I really like this property."

"Carina, please don't quit."

She sniffles. "I'll stay as long as you stay."

"Deal."

"You don't have the same name as your parents," I say. "Were you married?"

"No. It's my mom's maiden name. She and my dad weren't married yet when I was born, and my grandparents wouldn't let her give me his last name. I have come from a long line of controlling people."

"Well, there's no policy to control your love life anymore."

"They don't have to worry about me dating one of the landscapers here," she says. "We can't even get the same company to show up twice."

"But that last pool guy who came out . . ." I raise my eyebrows. "He could be a contender."

She shrugs. "Honestly, I'm more into the elevator repair guy. But the elevator hardly ever breaks, so I'll probably never see him again."

Vaughn laughs. "I'll break it for you on Monday."

A text pops up on my phone. "The police are here."

"I'll go down and meet them," she says. "Y'all have dealt with enough tonight. Enjoy the rest of your weekend."

I walk her to the door and hug her.

Vaughn comes up behind me and kisses my neck after she leaves. "I hope the owners are gone," I say. "The last thing we need is for them to run into the police on their way out."

"Carina can handle it." He nibbles my earlobe.

"She's not wrong about our landscaping vendor being unreliable. Do you have any unapproved landscapers you can call?"

"Yeah, I know a guy. I'll get you a new landscaper Monday morning, right after I break the elevator." His hands slide up my dress. "How do you feel about getting a dirty plumber tonight?"

"Does he have to be dirty?" I squirm against him as he pinches my nipples.

"You wouldn't like him if he wasn't." He trails one hand down my torso while the other goes to the back of my neck, pressing my cheek against the door.

"What's my role?"

"Sexiest real estate agent in town." His lower hand slides inside my panties.

"They sound like they could be good together."

"Oh, I have a feeling they're going to be a huge hit."

Vaughn

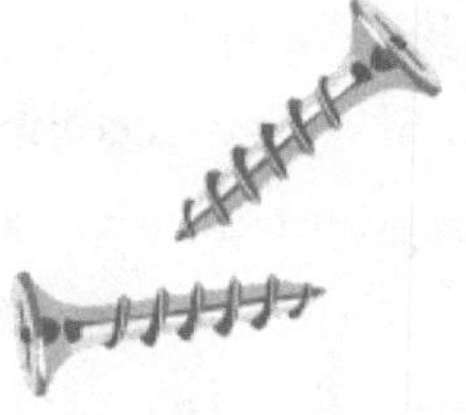

One Year Later

"Are you sure this pool party is a good idea?" I ask as I tape down the extension cord the deejay has stretched across the deck.

"Too late to talk her out of it now," Carina says. She tosses inflated white beach balls into the pool. "These are glow-in-the-dark. Isn't that cool? I can't wait for the sun to go down."

"So cool I hardly have words."

"Other properties host fun events for their tenants all the time," Landry says, right before she bites open a giant bag of leis and spreads them across a table. She knows I have a knife in my pocket

I would've gladly used to open that bag for her, but she uses her teeth anyway. I'll be pulling nylon flower petals out of the pool and the shrubs for a damn week after this.

"Sure," I say. "It just seems a little convenient that our first fun-filled tenant event happens to fall on the same weekend as Holden's graduation."

"His family thinks he wasted his time going to college, that he's chasing a dream that'll never come true. They're not even taking him out to dinner. Nobody did a damn thing for me when I got my degree either. I know how hard he's worked for this, and I know how much it sucks to have that accomplishment ignored. What does it hurt to have congratulations written on a cake? People like cake."

"So, you admit you're killing two birds with one stone."

"It's called working smarter, not harder."

"It's called finding a creative way to throw a deserving guy a much more impressive party than anyone else would've given him." I press my forehead to hers. "And he and all his friends, who I'm sure are just going to happen to stop by, are going to love it."

She allows me one quick kiss before she goes back to displaying party favors. "He only invited a few people. No one will even realize they don't live here."

"As long as nothing keeps us from heading to the beach tomorrow morning, you won't hear any complaints from me."

"The party ends at ten. We will be on the road early, and lying in the sun, listening to the waves before lunch tomorrow, I promise."

I step closer to her and whisper, "Do you want to go to the club for a while after the party ends?"

"We have to clean up. Besides, I don't need bruises on my ass at the beach."

"You could wear bottoms that actually cover your whole ass."

"If I owned any." She opens a box full of poppers and starts to set them out between the leis.

"There better not be confetti in those."

"What's confetti?"

"Landry."

"Vaughn."

Feedback screeches from the deejay's soundcheck. A stream of people flows through the pool gate. They swarm the table by Landry, grabbing at leis. Two guys cannonball into the pool. A beach ball bounces off my shoulder as Vonnie makes her entrance—wearing nothing but a bikini and a snake. There's no stopping this party now.

The sun beats down on my back as I run. Landry hasn't set her book down all day. Must be a good one. It's probably smut. I hope it's smut. I'll never understand why any man would have a problem with a woman in their life reading those books. Always seems to work out well for me.

I wade into the water to rinse the sweat off my body, and look back at her. The wind lifts the edges of the towel she's sitting on, but she doesn't so much as glance up from her book. Storms are rolling in. This will be our only day on the beach this weekend. It's supposed to start raining tonight and not stop until Monday. She says thunderstorms make perfect reading weather. She'll read. I'll alternate between TV and naps. We'll fuck in between. Not a bad way to spend a Sunday.

When I grab my towel to dry off, she stops reading and squints up at me as if she knows I'm going to say something.

"Are you hungry yet?"

"One more chapter."

That's what she always says. I sit next to her and let the sun dry the remaining salt water from my skin. The wind blows harder, loosening a hidden piece of confetti from her hair. It tumbles in the air for a moment before a gull dives down for it.

"Okay," she says, closing her book. "What are you in the mood for?"

"You."

"After you feed me, maybe."

"How long after? Are we talking in the parking lot or do I have to bring you all the way back to the house?"

"I'm not a parking lot kind of girl." She wraps a towel around her waist.

"But in the driveway or do we have to go inside?"

"Hmm, we've never had sex in your truck, have we?"

"Never. Not even on my birthday."

"It's too cold on your birthday."

"It's not cold today."

"We'll see."

That means no, but I smile like I think there's a chance. She smiles back because she knows I know better. We leave the beach, hand in hand, headed for food.

And whatever comes next.

Landry

Five Years Later

I SCREW THE BACK onto my second earring. "Put your phone down and look at me."

Vaughn drops his phone onto the bed. "I'm just checking to see if we've had any response to the listing yet."

"The tenants just moved out last week. It will be occupied again in no time. You need to focus on me tonight."

"We might need to think about selling that house instead of finding new tenants."

"This is our first broken lease. We knew it would happen at some point. We're fine. You need to remember how to relax."

"Relaxing stresses me out." He smiles, and I can see his shoulders release a little. "Fine," he says. "You have my undivided attention for the rest of the night."

"I still can't believe Holden invited us to the premier." I spin. "Are you sure this dress is better than the other one?"

"You look beautiful in both of them, but I like this one better."

"Because it's black?"

"What can I say? There's something about you in a black dress."

"I'm pretty sure the something about this one is its plunging neckline and missing back."

"Those are two of its best attributes, yes. What are you doing to it?"

"I'm using boob tape so I don't have a wardrobe malfunction in the theater."

"Way to ruin the perfect dress."

"Fix your tie and let's go be fancy."

I'm so proud of Holden for not giving up, no matter what his family said, but I'm also really happy for him because they showed up tonight. It doesn't matter how many times he said he didn't care one way or the other, I saw his face when his parents walked into the meet-and-greet social before the screening.

When the lights go down, I'm buzzing, and not just from the pre-show cocktails. Vaughn reaches for my hand.

The film is funny and heartwarming. Holden's voice rings clear, but this is the first time we're getting to see his characters brought to life. They're relatable. Almost too relatable. I lean over to Vaughn and whisper, "Do the construction foreman and that female architect he's always arguing with seem familiar to you?"

"I just keep thinking she's way too pretty to be that much of a pain in the ass."

"He pisses her off on purpose, but you just know they're dying to fuck each other."

"They'll probably end up together."

"Right?" I scoff. "Hollywood."

"Only in the movies."

He attempts to toss a piece of popcorn down my dress, but the boob tape keeps it out. I yank the fabric from my skin and let the kernel tumble down. "Oops."

"Exhibitionist."

"Perv."

"Love you."

"Love you more." I rest my head on his shoulder. He retrieves the popcorn from my dress, accidentally on purpose exposing my nipple. I cover it and reaffix the tape. He frowns.

"If one of them dies," I say. "I'm going to be so mad."

"It has a happy ending, I promise." He drops a fresh piece of popcorn at my neckline. "I've read the script."

I flick the popcorn off my chest and give him the look, the one that says *don't push your luck, buddy.* And then I snuggle against his shoulder so we can watch two insanely stubborn people fall madly in love. What a fucking cliché.

Thank you so much for visiting The Nouveau!
I hope you enjoyed getting to know all the characters who live and work in this fabulous community.

Please come back soon for book 2, **Landscaping & Leasing**. This is Carina's chance to be the heroine. I think we can agree she's earned a love story of her own, right? https://books2read.com/NaughtyAtTheNouveau2 Read on for a sneak peek!

If you haven't done so yet, please visit my website at https://indiesparks.net, where you can find all my books. And don't forget to **sign up for my newsletter** when the invitation appears. You will receive free stories for subscribing, and you'll always receive the latest information about my books, including the raunch-com duet that made me fall in love with writing these steamy, fun companion reads: Your Boss Says Hi! and Your Trainer Says Hi!, and upcoming signings/appearances.

EXCERPT from Landscaping & Leasing:

I speak without looking up because I just need to finish typing this email right quick. "I'll be with you in just one moment."

His voice sparks embers at the base of my spine. "Please, take your time. I'm a little early. Traffic was light."

Please let me be having some sort of neurological episode. Anything would be better than having him actually standing in my office. I cautiously let my eyes drift from my computer screen toward the man whose voice has caused the tremor in my core. "Declan? You own Rough Hands Landscaping?"

"Guilty."

"I didn't accuse you of anything. Yet." My tone has shifted from casual to caustic. I didn't even realize I was still angry with him, but fuck if I don't want to hurl a stapler at his gorgeous face right now.

He's not smiling, just giving me that look—the one that says he's up for a challenge, eager to see my next move. "Hi, Carina."

"Did you know it was going to be me?"

"I had a hunch when my office manager told me I was meeting with a woman named Carina."

"I wish I'd confirmed your name. You couldn't have called to give me a heads up? That sounds about right."

"Can I take you to lunch?"

"I already hired your company, Dec. No need to schmooze me to get my business."

"I know. But I always like to swing by and meet new customers after the first time my crews come out." He has a seat in one of the two chairs on the other side of my desk, makes himself comfortable. "So, how'd we do?"

"You have eyes. Feel free to walk the grounds and see for yourself."

"I'll do that before I leave, but as the customer, what is your impression of the job we did?"

"Your prices are a little steep." I definitely should've hired Vaughn's guy. Our maintenance supervisor knows a vendor for everything, but his landscaping guy gave me a bad vibe, so when the foreman for Rough Hands Landscaping walked in the next day with a business card and a price sheet, I hired them on the spot. We were in a bind. I made a snap decision. And now I'm staring at the biggest mistake of my life . . . one my body would like to make again, but my head is too smart for round two.

"We do good work, and I pay my guys a fair wage. We're fully insured and have well-maintained, reliable equipment. Everything comes at a cost, but I like to think the quality of our service is worth it."

In my head I'm mimicking him: *but I like to think the quality of our service . . .* "He tilts his head and narrows his hazel eyes as if he can hear my mocking thoughts. The sight of his jawline could still give a sketch artist an orgasm. But I'm not a sketch artist. At best, it has my panties a little wet. Okay, maybe my pussy has clenched a few times, but that means nothing. And my nipples were hard long before he walked in. Landry set the air conditioner to arctic blast this morning, and I keep forgetting to turn it down. Or up, I mean. I think.

Fuck, how am I supposed to know up from down with my greatest heartbreak sitting across from me, radiating all his villainous sex appeal, wielding that shit like a weapon?

"As far as I can tell, your guys did a good job. They showed up on time, so that's a plus. Hell, the fact that y'all showed up at all is damn plus." I exhale through laughter. I'm no good at the tough girl act, and Declan always saw right through me, anyway.

"Yeah, I keep hearing that from customers. I'd like to stand out for more than the bare minimum, but it seems my competition is setting the bar low these days."

His eyebrows lift as if he intended some double entendre, like he's asking an unspoken question. If he thinks I'm going to give away anything about my current personal life, he's delusional. "Well, so far you're ahead of the rest."

Oh, give me a break with that smug smile. He knows I didn't mean him personally. "Your company, that is." Never hurts to clarify in moments like this. With a man like him.

"Good to know."

Landry comes back in from her lunch break, carrying shopping bags. I wonder why she didn't take them up to her apartment, but I don't have to wonder for long. "I got you a pre-sent," she sing-songs, still lost in her post-shopping happy place, completely unaware of Declan's long legs manspreading in front of my desk.

She has the sex toy halfway out when she finally spots him and drops it back into the depths of the bag. I don't have to see the other half to know my present is a two-part toy: a clit sucker on one end and a thruster on the other.

We talked about them all morning, and we maybe watched a few videos just to be sure we fully understood how they worked. But I never dreamed she was going to buy me one on her lunch break!

Landry's disappointed in me because I abandoned all dating sites over the weekend. I've *given up on love* as she put it. She said if I wasn't going to try to land a real boyfriend, I at least needed the top-of-the-line rechargeable model. That was the comment that sent us down the deluxe dildo rabbit hole to begin with.

Now, I apparently own one, and my ex saw it for the first time right along with me. Guess he probably doesn't have any further questions about his competition in that regard.

"I didn't realize you were going shopping," I say.

Her smile is part apology, part intrigue. "Hi," she says, extending her hand to Declan.

I intervene to complete the introductions. "This is our manager, Landry. Landry, this is Declan, he owns the new landscaping company I hired last week."

"It's so nice to have a company that shows up when they're scheduled. And I can't remember the last time an owner followed up in person," she gushes. "You're blowing your competition out of the water."

He glances at the bag in her hand. "I sure hope so."

Landscaping & Leasing: https://books2read.com/Naughtyat
TheNouveau2

Acknowledgements

My thanks go out to all the usual suspects for helping me bring this book into the world: trusted and treasured beta readers, my fabulous ARC team, my PA, and countless author friends who cheer and commiserate as needed. I'm not listing them individually here, not because I appreciate them any less, but because I've named so many of them before, and I want to offer a special thanks to strangers for this one.

That's right, I said strangers. Thank you to all the bawdy older women who've shed the burden of other people's opinions. Thank you to the bold and passionate people who live out loud on their own terms and love who they love with fuck-all concern for who thinks what about it. Thank you to the ones who've been hurt but refuse to let it make them hard, reminding us all that love can still win.

And thank you for reading with wild abandon!
It's your right.
Don't let anyone take it without a fight.